TEMPTING THE BILLIONAIRE

THE SHERBROOKES OF NEWPORT

CHRISTINA TETREAULT

Tempting The Billionaire, ©2020 by Christina Tetreault
Published by Christina Tetreault
Cover Designer: Amanda Walker
Editing: Hot Tree Editing

Digital ISBN: 978-1-7329429-6-7

Print ISBN: 978-1-7329429-7-4

ONE

SLIDING OPEN THE GLASS DOORS, Courtney stepped outside, closed her eyes, and took in a deep breath of fresh air. Nothing else in the world smelled like the air in Hawaii, and she should know, considering all the places she'd visited. For a few minutes, she stood there with her eyes closed and let the sun warm her face while the sound of the ocean washed over her.

Paradise. There really was no other word for the island. How could you call it anything else? The temperature never dipped too low, unlike in Boston where the whopping temperature this morning when she stepped on the plane was twenty-eight degrees. At the same time, the island rarely saw temps go higher than ninety. As if the wonderful weather wasn't enough, Hawaii had gorgeous beaches and water perfect for swimming and surfing.

Yep, as much as she loved New England and its four seasons, she adored Hawaii. It was by far her favorite place to retreat to when she wanted to get away. Actually, more than once she'd considered moving out here permanently. Each time, though, the fact that such a move would take her so far away from her family stopped her. Instead, she settled for owning a suite at the Sherbrooke Hawaiian Village Resort and coming whenever she could.

Unfortunately, the past seven months had been hectic thanks to both family and work obligations, making a visit impossible. For the next two weeks, she planned to soak up as much sunshine as she could before heading back to Providence and diving into her new position at the Helping Hands Foundation while at the same helping with her uncle Warren's reelection campaign.

Not that he needed much help. Even though the other party had yet to even hold their primaries, political polls were predicting her uncle would win a second term, a fact that didn't come at all as a surprise. Throughout his presidency, Uncle Warren had maintained a high approval rating, and since he took office, the economy was doing well. Still, the man was her uncle, and she wanted to help him, so whether or not his campaign needed her, she'd be there.

The opening to Tchaikovsky's 1812 Overture reached her out on the balcony, and Courtney opened her eyes. Glancing inside, she considered letting the call go to voice mail. If it was important, the caller could leave a message, and she'd call them back later. On the other hand, the responsible thing to do would be to take the call now and handle the matter before she did anything else. And if Courtney was anything, it was responsible. Sometimes maybe even a little too responsible, according to her younger sister, Juliette, who often insisted she needed to be more spontaneous and fun loving. Unlike when it came to several of her cousins and sister, those two words never appeared in a sentence alongside the name Courtney Belmont.

She left the doors open when she stepped back inside and

retrieved the cell phone from her purse. She expected the call to be from one of three people: her mom, Juliette, or her best friend, Meg, since they called her the most. A glance at the screen showed it was instead from her cousin Leah.

"Hey, are you around this upcoming weekend? Gavin and I are heading to Providence. I thought we could get together. I haven't even seen your new place yet," Leah greeted.

While Leah and Gavin called Connecticut home, Gavin's daughter, Erin, lived in Providence. Rather than waste time driving back and forth, Gavin kept an apartment in the city, and he and Leah usually stayed there when it was his weekend to have Erin.

"Sorry, no. I'm in Hawaii." If she was at home, she'd love to spend some time with her cousin. With so much else going on, including her move from Boston to Providence, she had spent little time with any of her cousins. The same was true of her siblings.

"Did you go straight from the reception to the airport?"

Leah wasn't too far off. After her brother Scott's wedding reception, she'd stayed at her parents' house before driving into Boston early this morning to catch her flight. "No, I flew out today."

"Good timing. It's supposed to snow again tonight. Hopefully, they're right this time and we only get two inches."

The previous week the meteorologists had predicted they'd get a mere inch or two before the snow changed into rain. They'd been off by about eight inches.

"Hawaii. Nice choice. I wouldn't mind being someplace warm right now. When will you be home?" Leah asked.

"The seventeenth. I want to be there for election night." There wasn't a doubt in Courtney's mind that her cousin Brett would win the special election being held to fill the vacant Senate seat on December 19, and she wanted to be there to congratulate him when he did.

"Can you believe my brother still refuses to admit he's going to win? Every poll has him ahead of Gina Hammond. There is no way he'll lose."

Courtney agreed. However she, like everyone in the family, knew changing Brett's mind about anything was impossible. So until they counted all the ballots and declared Brett the winner, he'd remain open to the possibility that he might lose.

"Then I guess we'll get to say 'we told you so' on election night," Courtney replied before moving the conversation on to something she'd wanted to ask Leah Saturday but couldn't since Gavin had stayed by her side all day. "Any idea when Gavin will ask you to marry him?"

Thanks to Gavin's daughter, Leah knew he'd bought an engagement ring months ago. Despite having it, though, he hadn't popped the question, and the wait was driving her crazy. In Leah's shoes, Courtney would be going a little nutty too.

"No clue." Leah's exasperation traveled through the phone. "But I've made a decision."

Sitting inside and talking on the phone while in Hawaii made about as much sense as wearing a bikini while skiing, so Courtney grabbed a bottled water from the kitchen and headed back onto the balcony. Having a well-stocked kitchen waiting for her thanks to a single phone call was just one of the many perks of owning a suite inside a hotel.

"If he doesn't propose before the end of the month, I'm going to ask him to marry me on New Year's Eve," Leah explained.

Courtney unscrewed the cap and took a sip as she sat down. "Why wait until then? Do it now."

"I.... Honestly, I don't know. Waiting until the end of the month feels right."

Courtney could almost hear her cousin shrugging back on the East Coast.

"I know it makes no sense. But I'm going to wait and see what happens. If he hasn't asked by New Year's Eve, I'll ask him before the party," Leah continued, referring to the annual New Year's Eve bash the Sherbrooke family had been holding every year for decades at Cliff House in Newport.

Part of her hoped Gavin proposed before the end of the month, because if he'd bought a ring and told his daughter, he obviously wanted to do it. At the same time, she liked the idea of Leah taking control of the situation and asking him. Regardless of which way it happened, Courtney was happy her cousin had such a great man in her life. Considering the creeps she'd dated in the past, Leah deserved to be with someone who adored her. And no question about it, Gavin Kincaid was crazy about Leah.

"Well, if he asks before I see you, call me."

"Don't worry, I will. Have fun on vacation, and I'll see you on election night."

After ending the call, Courtney remained outside enjoying the view and thinking about how she wanted to spend the next few hours. Did she want to go down to the beach and work on her tan? It'd been a while since she was in the ocean. She could grab her surfboard and head for the waves. Or did she want to take a dip in one of the many hotel pools and then sit in the sun with a fruity umbrella-decorated drink? As much as she loved the beach and the ocean, between her late night on Saturday and her long flight today, she was tired. A relaxing afternoon doing nothing more taxing than lifting a drink and maybe reading a book seemed like a better way to kick off her vacation. Tomorrow she'd grab her surfboard or snorkel and enjoy the ocean.

While there were certainly downsides to calling a hotel home, in her opinion the perks outweighed them. First, she never needed to worry about employing staff to maintain the grounds or the interior. When she used the suite, the hotel staff took care of vacuuming and making the bed just like they did in the rest of the hotel. Second, she had access to room service and all the other amenities the hotel offered, including a five-star spa and both freshwater and saltwater swimming pools. Really, with so many benefits, unless she moved out here permanently, it made no sense for her to purchase any property.

Unlike a lot of her friends, when it came to swimwear, Courtney's middle name was modesty. So after changing into one of the swimsuits she'd bought specifically for this trip, a crimson tankini, she headed up to the rooftop pool armed with everything she needed to spend a few hours in the sun.

Although not the largest of the pools at the hotel, the one on the rooftop allowed you to swim while looking out over Waikiki Beach and the Pacific Ocean. Besides the pool, there was a hot tub for relaxing. If water wasn't your thing or you wanted a break from it, there were padded lounge chairs, several small tables, and a full-service bar. After a quick but refreshing lap in the pool, Courtney snagged an empty table since there were no vacant lounge chairs and ordered a Mai Tai, because when it came to tropical drinks with little umbrellas, it didn't get much better.

"He really is too yummy for words," the thirty-something-year-old brunette sitting at the next table over said to her companion. Although Courtney couldn't place her or the woman who had to be either a sister or cousin based on the resemblance, both of them looked vaguely familiar.

"Who?" the platinum blonde wearing a bikini that left nothing to the imagination asked.

Courtney pulled the latest book by one of her favorite mystery writers from her bag and ignored the conversation. Or at least she tried.

"Scott Belmont," the brunette replied.

Courtney pressed her lips together to keep from laughing. She couldn't deny her older brother was handsome, but to hear the woman describe him as too yummy for words was downright funny.

"According to the *Star Insider* website, he got married yesterday," the brunette continued.

She mentally groaned. Courtney, like most of her relatives, hated the *Star Insider*, a popular tabloid television show, because nine times out of ten the stories they reported were pure trash. Even when they got some of the details correct, they embellished them to get a bigger wow factor. If there was a story about Scott on the site now, she didn't expect it to be any different.

From the corner of her eye, she saw the woman look back at her smartphone.

"Scott Belmont, the nephew of President Sherbrooke, married his longtime girlfriend, Paige Foster, Saturday in a small and intimate ceremony surrounded by family and friends," the brunette read from the popular tabloid website.

Courtney stifled a laugh when she heard the article describe the ceremony as small and intimate. She couldn't help herself. Since the guest list had included more than one hundred people, most individuals wouldn't consider her brother's wedding an intimate affair. However, considering that the groom was the great-grandson of the late hotel magnate Gabriel Sherbrooke and the grandson of former newspaper giant Thomas Belmont, it had been a small affair with only family and close friends in attendance.

"Readers might recall the two met last year at a Helping Hands Bachelor auction in Providence where Ms. Foster bid on and won four dates with Mr. Belmont. This marriage marks the eighth Sherbrooke wedding in less than four years." The woman finished reading the article and set down the device. "I almost went to that fundraiser. If I had, I would have paid anything to win Scott or his cousin."

The platinum blonde laughed and reached for her drink. "As if you would've been able to win either of them, Kylie. I read somewhere that Paige Foster's grandfather owns Foster Oil, and the winner of Scott's cousin bid more than one hundred thousand dollars."

Courtney wanted to tell them the article was wrong. While Paige's grandfather was the owner of Foster Oil, she didn't rely on any of his money. In fact, she worked as a nurse, and the night of the auction she hadn't bid on Scott. Her aunt had tugged Paige's arm in the air when the auctioneer asked if there were any more bids. The same aunt had dished out the money later. But if she set the record straight, people would wonder how she knew, and she'd prefer to stay under the radar and not be recognized as a member of the Sherbrooke family— something she could usually manage since, unlike a lot of her relatives, she didn't have the signature Sherbrooke blue eyes or light hair. She found avoiding any outrageous behavior helped too.

"If the foundation holds another auction, Bella, we should go," Kylie said.

The event had been such a success that her mom, the current director of the foundation, was considering holding it again. Courtney had mixed feelings about it, and now that she worked for the foundation, she planned to have an in-depth conversation with her mom when she got back.

"Sounds like a plan. Mom might even—" Bella stopped and pulled her sunglasses off. "Is that J.T. Williamson over there by the bar?"

As if they had a mind of their own, Courtney's eyes glanced at the bar, but unlike her neighbor, she kept her sunglasses on. No need to give away that she was staring at the guy if he happened to look this way.

It wasn't hard to pick out the man in question. Joshua Thomas Williamson, better known to his fans as J.T., was the epitome of the term Hollywood heartthrob. If a list existed of all the necessary requirements, he'd be able to put a check mark next to all of them. Dark hair? Yep, he had that. Chiseled jaw? Yes. Tall? Courtney estimated he was about 6'0 or 6'1. Broad shoulders? Most definitely. Sexy barely there beard? Check.

Yep, the guy was the total package, and he knew it. The only people who'd possibly appeared on more tabloid covers than him were two of her cousins before they met and married their wives.

"Yes, and I think he's looking this way," her brunette neighbor answered.

Kylie, the woman she was still trying to place, was right. J.T. Williamson, perhaps the biggest playboy in Hollywood, was glancing in their direction. For perhaps the first time, Courtney wished she had on a swimsuit more like her neighbors', because she'd never catch his attention dressed in her modest tankini, especially with the platinum blonde bombshell at the next table. And even though she never went for the playboy types, man, Courtney wanted to catch the attention of this one for reasons she couldn't identify.

"THANKS." Josh accepted the drink and surveyed the area. There was no shortage of beautiful women on the rooftop this afternoon. He'd come to Hawaii for some rest and relaxation, something he needed now that he'd finished work on his most recent project. While he had perhaps the best job on the planet, even he needed a break sometimes—especially after working with Nicole Sutton for the past six months. Anyone who watched them on screen together would never guess it, but he couldn't stand Nicole. Thankfully, he'd learned early in his career how to put aside his personal feelings and get the job done. Josh didn't know how Nicole felt about him, but since she never sought him out when they weren't working together, he assumed she wasn't his biggest fan either.

His eyes passed over a brunette and a platinum blonde. Both were pretty with gorgeous bodies—the type of women he usually spent his time with. Considering the way they were both looking at him, either would be up for a little fun while he was here. Something he wouldn't object to if the right woman came along, because a person could only surf and swim so much every day.

Josh put them in the "maybe" category and continued his survey of the guests gathered around the pool. At first, his eyes passed over the occupant at the table next to the blonde. But then, as if attached to a rubber band, they snapped back. Unlike most of the women, including her two neighbors, she wasn't wearing a barely there bikini. Instead, she had on a modest swimsuit. Her brown hair hung past her shoulders, and she had a sexy librarian look about her. He didn't usually go for her type. Instead, he went for the platinum blonde with the large breasts spilling out of her top who was smiling at him. He'd always had a thing for large breasts. Today, the sexy librarian had his full attention.

With his drink in hand, Josh headed for the brunette who was applying sunscreen to her shoulders.

"Do you mind if I join you?" He could feel her neighbors' eyes on him. "There aren't many places left to sit." If there was an extra chair at her neighbors' table, he knew they'd be offering it up right now.

Her sunglasses made it impossible for him to determine the color of her eyes when she glanced up at him. "Not at all," she said, moving her cell phone closer to her side of the table. "It is busy up here this afternoon."

Rarely did he run into a person who didn't know him, but

just in case, he'd introduce himself. So after sitting down, Josh extended his hand across the table. "My name's Josh. I hope I'm not bothering you." While professionally he went by J.T. and some of his friends called him that, in situations like this he preferred to use his given name.

She accepted his hand and smiled. "Courtney. And you're not."

Now that he was closer, he realized he'd been wrong. Her hair wasn't brown but auburn with a few blonde highlights. Not only that, she looked familiar, but he couldn't pinpoint from where. Wherever he knew her from, he was confident she wasn't an actress he'd ever worked with, because if they'd worked together, he would have remembered her. Maybe if she removed her sunglasses, he could figure it out.

"Have we met before?"

A second or two passed before Courtney responded. "No, I don't think so."

Maybe it would come to him later, because even though she didn't think they'd met, something told him he'd seen her somewhere. Perhaps they'd attended the same party or fundraiser. He attended so many, they all blurred together after a while. The same might be true for her. "Are you here for work or a vacation?"

She reached for her drink and took a sip. "A much needed vacation before I start a new job in Providence. You?"

Providence was a place he knew well. He'd grown up in Rhode Island and frequently went back to visit his family and friends. "As in Providence, Rhode Island?" There might be other states with cities named Providence, but if there were, he'd never heard of them.

"Yep."

While it was possible she was relocating to the area, if she was starting a new job in Providence, there was a good chance she was from New England. That possibility nudged something in his memory, but he couldn't quite put his finger on it. "Great city. My brother Evan lives there. And my dad is in East Greenwich."

Two hours later, they remained in the same spot, enjoying a second round of cocktails. Fans wanting a photo with him and an autograph had interrupted them several times. If it bothered Courtney, she never let on. Most of the time, it didn't bother him either. Today though, with each interruption, his annoyance grew. Rarely did he sit down and have an enjoyable conversation with a woman unless she was a relative. Usually when he went up to a woman like he had today, they didn't want or expect an in-depth conversation from him. Some just wanted to be seen with him. Others wanted him to get them into a place they otherwise wouldn't get invited. Most of the women he spent time with only wanted sex, which meant they went from saying hello to removing each other's clothes in a short amount of time.

Nothing Courtney said or did suggested she wanted anything from him but a conversation. They'd discussed their favorite spots in Rhode Island and how she wasn't looking forward to the cold weather when she returned to New England. They even talked about books. He couldn't help but bring up the topic when he spotted the novel by one of his favorite authors on the table.

"I'm ready for a change of scenery," he said before he finished his second mojito. While it was possible she wasn't on vacation alone, he doubted she would have spent two hours here with him if she had a boyfriend on the island. "Do you want to join me for dinner? Afterward, maybe we can stop in Ka Pua."

Normally when he asked a woman out, she answered immediately. Not Courtney. A few seconds passed before she nodded. "Sounds good. I've gotten enough sun for now, anyway. And I am getting hungry." She picked up her book and tossed it in the bag near her feet. "Depending on where we go, we'll want to make reservations. What do you feel like eating?"

When it came to food, he ate anything. Even as a kid, while his siblings refused to eat certain foods, he cleaned his plate regardless of what was on it and often finished what they didn't want. "I'm open to suggestions."

"Takumi over on Ala Moana Boulevard has phenomenal sushi. If we go there, we'll need a reservation. Or..." Courtney tapped her fingernails against her cell phone. "Or we could go to Mistral."

He wasn't familiar with the first restaurant she mentioned, but he'd eaten at the second, which was just one of the many in the hotel complex. "Let's go to Mistral. Do you want me to call them when I get back to my room and make a reservation?" One of the perks of being so well known, he never had to worry about getting a reservation when he called, regardless of how popular or exclusive the establishment.

"I'll take care of it." She slipped the straps of her bag over her shoulder and stood.

"If you can't get us a reservation, call me," he said before rattling off his number.

"It shouldn't be a problem." She saved the information in her cell anyway before giving him her number. "Where would you like to meet?"

It didn't escape him that she wasn't giving out the number of her hotel room. He didn't blame her, because having dinner in a public place with someone you'd just met was one thing. Telling the individual to come to your room was another. In fact, it was something he wouldn't want his younger sister doing in a similar situation.

"How about in the lobby in forty minutes?" It didn't get much more public than that.

"Perfect. I'll see you in a little while," Courtney replied.

Josh watched her walk away. Actually, he wasn't the only guy out there who watched her. Before she reached the door, Paris Novak, a former runway model who had recently made the move into acting, called out to her, and Courtney stopped to chat. Was that why she looked familiar? Paris and her husband, Seth Vallencourt, regularly threw parties at their home. He'd attended several, and if Courtney knew Paris, perhaps she'd gone to one and he'd seen her there. If it didn't come to him before they met downstairs, he'd have to ask her if she attended any of their parties, because he knew he'd seen her somewhere, and at the moment her connection to Paris was the only clue he had.

TWO

Courtney's conversation with Paris, her cousin's sister-in-law, meant she had less time than she would have liked to get ready. Even with the little setback, she reached the outdoor lobby before Josh, and at the moment she was watching the assortment of fish swim in one of the several koi ponds located in the hotel complex.

"Oh, my God, Molly. J.T. Williamson is here. I can't believe he's staying at the same hotel as us," a female voice blurted.

Courtney glanced at the teenager, whom she estimated to be around sixteen, standing a few feet away. Then her gaze drifted in the direction the girls were looking. On the rooftop in nothing but swim shorts and sunglasses, she'd thought Josh was hot. She'd been wrong. Dressed in khaki-colored pants—the maître d' at Mistral wouldn't let you through the door in shorts—and a dress shirt with the top two buttons left open, the man set a new world record in male hotness.

"He's coming this way. We have to ask him for an auto-graph," Molly, who had to be the other teen's identical twin, replied. Before her sister could agree, Molly grabbed her hand,

and the two headed in Josh's direction. They intercepted him as he approached the gorgeous parrot named Red who was hanging out on his perch and occasionally calling out greetings to guests.

From where she stood, Courtney couldn't hear their conversation. But Josh signed the sleeve of both girls' T-shirts before posing for pictures with each of them. Once he'd satisfied their requests, they ran off, both focused on their cell phones as they typed away. Courtney imagined they were sending the pictures off to their friends back home. With the young fans gone, Josh turned his eyes on her and smiled as he closed the remaining distance between them.

Thanks to the media and her cousin, she knew all about Josh's well-earned reputation. Except for one long-term relationship a few years ago, he bounced from one woman to another like a tennis ball going over a net. Sometimes he'd spend a Friday night with a model and then wake up Sunday morning with a well-known actress. Never in her life had she gone out with such a man.

Actually, she didn't date much in general. When she did, the men were often individuals more interested in using their connection to her to further their careers or social standings. Even if her romantic life wasn't so pathetic, she knew a man like Josh, who couldn't commit for more than a night, wasn't the type she wanted to waste her time on. Or at least usually she wouldn't want to waste her time on.

Lately, she found herself bored and frustrated. For the past couple of years, she'd been watching her family members find *the* one. Not only hadn't she found the one, but she hadn't even been out with anyone in over eight months. While inviting Josh Williamson back to her suite wouldn't get her any closer to finding someone she might spend her life with, it would make her vacation a little more exciting. And much like sex, excitement was another thing her life lacked. Unlike her younger sister, Courtney was the queen of predictability and responsibility. This afternoon, though, her sister's voice insisting there was nothing wrong with having fun as long as you were responsible came through loud and clear. Unfortunately, she'd also heard her cousin Trent telling her to stay as far away from his friend as possible—something she found amusing, considering how similar his behavior had once been to Josh's.

By the pool, she almost suggested they have dinner in her suite but in the end decided to err on the side of caution. Right now she wished she hadn't.

"Hey. You look beautiful. I hope you haven't been waiting too long." He kissed her cheek.

Around them, fans snapped pictures and called out his name. She was used to professional photographers taking her picture if they spotted her with her sister or a cousin. She wasn't used to random people whipping out their cell phones and snapping photos though.

"No, I just got here."

Josh placed his hand on her back. The warmth from it seeped into her bare skin, then spread like a wildfire, making her wish he had more than just his hand pressed against her body.

"Did you have any trouble getting us a reservation?" he asked as they started walking.

When your family owned the entire hotel complex, getting a reservation for dinner was never a problem. "Nope, we're all set."

Although she was no stranger to the French restaurant, the maître d' didn't recognize her when they entered. "Good evening and welcome to Mistral. Do you have a reservation this evening?"

"It should be under Courtney Belmont." She intentionally hadn't given Josh her full name up by the pool. For once in her life, she'd wanted to know the man across the table from her wasn't there only because of who made up her family tree.

"The table you requested, Ms. Belmont, is ready. If you'll please follow me."

Another perk of being a part of the Sherbrooke family, not only could she get a reservation at any restaurant she desired, she could get the exact spot she wanted in the place. If she'd been with almost anyone else, she wouldn't have cared where they sat. Tonight she'd rather not have a repeat of when they'd been near the pool and fans thought nothing of intruding on them and requesting an autograph or picture.

The maître d' pulled out a chair and waited for Courtney to sit before handing her a large leather-bound menu. "Enjoy your meal. If you require anything, please don't hesitate to ask."

Across the table, Josh studied her, and she could see the gears turning in his head. By the pool, he'd asked if they'd met because she looked familiar. When she told him no, she hadn't been lying since they'd never been introduced. However, he'd attended her cousin Trent's wedding, so it wasn't like she only knew him because he appeared in Hollywood blockbusters.

"Are you related to Scott Belmont and Trent Sherbrooke?" he asked once they were alone.

After tonight, they might never see each other again, so if she lied, he would never know the difference. On too many occasions, though, she'd seen how what seemed like a simple lie could backfire on you in the long run.

"Guilty as charged. Trent's my cousin, and Scott is my brother."

"Explains why you look so familiar. I must have seen you at Trent and Addie's wedding. Still can*not* believe he's not only married but a father."

You're not the only one. Courtney adored her cousin, but— at least until he met his wife—she'd never thought of him as husband and father material. Despite her previous beliefs, she'd never seen him happier.

"I read your brother married the woman who bought him at the bachelor auction." Josh picked up his menu and opened it. "Once they went out on their four dates, my brother couldn't get rid of the woman who bought him at the auction."

She'd attended the event but didn't remember who'd claimed his brother Evan on stage.

"Not only did she call him for months, but she'd randomly show up at his condo."

Now she really wished she remembered who'd won Evan that night. When she returned home, she might need to look up the information. "Is she still bothering him?" Courtney glanced at the entrées listed to see if there were any new additions since her last visit.

"Evan hasn't heard from her in about four months. I'm hoping it stays that way. The calls and visits were getting to his girlfriend."

"I don't blame her. I wouldn't like it either."

"Does the foundation plan to hold the event again? It sounded like it was a huge success."

There was no denying the auction had been a big money-maker for the foundation. However, she had mixed feelings about the idea of someone buying dates with an individual. "The foundation hasn't decided yet. If we do, are you interested in taking part?" Smiling, she set aside her menu. "Because if you are, I can put in a good word for you."

"No, I'm all set, but thanks for thinking of me."

"If you change your mind, just let me know. Who knows, you might end up like my brother and meet your future wife."

Before they could continue, their waitress arrived to take their order. Although the woman remained professional and didn't request an autograph or a photo, it was easy to see she not only knew who Josh was but was also a fan.

Josh waited until they were alone to speak again. "Is the new job you're starting in Providence at the foundation?"

She nodded. "Mom has wanted me to join her for a few years. When Rose stepped down as chief development officer, Mom asked me to take over the position. I'm looking forward to it when I get home."

JOSH'S EARS were still ringing from the loud music inside the club when they entered the nearly deserted lobby holding hands. His ears weren't the only part of his body suffering. After watching Courtney's body move for the past few hours, he was well past ready to feel her move underneath him, or over him for that matter. Since he didn't know in which part of the resort she was staying, he stopped where he'd met her earlier in the evening and said a silent thank-you there were not any fans around. They'd made it through dinner with no interruptions. Thanks to the mass of people inside and the lighting, he'd gone mostly unnoticed in the club as well.

"My body is still on East Coast time, so I should be tired, but I'm not," Courtney said as she moved so they were facing each other. She placed her hand on his chest and played with a button on his shirt as she raked her teeth across her bottom lip. "Do you want to come upstairs for a drink or dessert?"

There was a hint of uncertainty in her voice, suggesting she didn't ask men back to her hotel room on a regular basis. He didn't know why she was doing it now, but he wasn't going to turn down her offer. Josh moved in closer and placed his hands on her waist before he lowered his lips toward hers but stopped before he made contact.

"Love to." Josh brushed his lips across hers and reminded himself they were still in a public place. While the lobby wasn't busy like it had been earlier, there were still guests strolling through. He didn't care if he showed up on the cover of *Today Magazine* making out with a woman. It had happened before, and it would happen again. But the little he'd learned about Courtney so far told him she would. He wasn't a saint, but he never intentionally did something to make someone else uncomfortable.

When he ended the kiss, she reached for his hand and led him through the lobby, past one of the outdoor pools, and to the Hokulani Tower. Whenever possible, he reserved a room in that part of the resort as well. On this trip, he'd snagged the Kauoaeo Suite on the twelfth floor. Rather than lead him to one of the three elevators situated just inside the building, Courtney turned the corner and stopped at a single elevator. After she entered her access code, the door opened. Unlike the one he rode down in earlier, this elevator only accessed the top two floors of the tower and the rooftop.

He waited until the doors closed before pulling her close and bringing his lips down on hers. Unlike in the lobby, he moved his mouth over hers, urging her to open for him. Courtney didn't keep him waiting long, and when her lips parted, he thrust his tongue inside. At the same time, her hands inched down his back. They stopped for a moment when they reached his waist as if she was trying to make a decision. Then she moved them lower until they settled on his ass. Immediately other parts of his body took notice. He thought he'd been uncomfortable before. Now the word took on a whole new meaning.

Somehow he heard the chime when the elevator doors opened despite his heartbeat throbbing in his ears. If Courtney heard it, she gave no indication. Tearing his mouth away, Josh nodded toward the open doors once she opened her eyes.

Without saying a word, she reached for his hand and stepped out of the elevator and into a living room larger than his entire suite. While furnished in a similar manner, it was obvious the room contained a lot of personal touches, meaning only members of the Sherbrooke family used this part of the hotel. Hell, since it was where Courtney was staying, the suite might belong to her. She had mentioned earlier that Hawaii was one of her favorite places to visit. Maybe he'd ask her later.

"Do you want to order dessert now or later?" Much like downstairs, a hint of uncertainty lurked in her voice.

Let her set the pace. You've got all night. Despite his discomfort, he wanted her to enjoy their time too, even if it meant letting her take control.

"Whatever you want."

She didn't answer with words. Instead, she pressed her lips against the side of his neck and slowly seared a path up. When she reached his earlobe, she ran her tongue across it before closing her lips around it and sucking. Instantly the images of her doing the same on another part of his body filled his head, and he groaned as he cupped her breast in his right hand. Through the thin fabric of her sundress, her nipple pressed into his palm. He let his hand linger there for a few moments as he learned the shape and feel of her breast before he slipped his finger inside her bra.

Releasing his ear, Courtney's lips came down on his as her fingers worked to undo the buttons on his shirt. When she finished, she pushed his shirt off his shoulders and pulled away, dislodging his hand.

The words "one of us is overdressed" were almost of out his mouth when her eyes met his, and she reached for the zipper of her dress. Although he wanted nothing more than to assist her, he kept his arms by his side and waited. Thankfully, he didn't have to wait long. Once the zipper was down, she slipped the straps from her shoulders and let the fabric fall to the floor before releasing the clasp of her bra and tossing it aside. His eyes dropped from her eyes to her shoulders and then to her breasts. He allowed his gaze to linger there while thinking about all the ways he'd pleasure them before moving on. This time he allowed his hands to travel with his eyes. He felt her sharp intake of breath as his fingers made a path down her ribs and over her stomach toward the edge of her lace panties. Josh paused for a moment, giving her the opportunity to tell him to stop. When she remained silent, he traveled lower, pushed the material aside, and slipped one finger inside her.

"Do you prefer white or red?" Courtney sat up and looked over at him.

"Let's go with white."

Leaning over, she kissed him before standing up. Rather than leave though, she pulled open the glass doors leading outside. "I don't know about you, but I'm hungry. Do you want me to order room service or just get us something from the kitchen?"

After all their physical activity since coming upstairs, he was ready for an entire meal, never mind a snack. "Whatever you have in the kitchen is fine."

Grabbing a short bathrobe from the closet, she slipped it on and, much to his disappointment, tied it closed. Then she stopped alongside the bed and leaned down. "Be right back," she promised before kissing him again.

Unable to help himself, Josh reached under the robe and touched her. At first, she closed her eyes and allowed him to tease her. He was about to pull her back into bed when she stepped away. "Food first."

He watched her leave the room before flopping onto his back and staring at the ceiling as the ocean breeze cooled his heated body. Based on the way she'd invited him upstairs, he'd expected her to be a passive lover. There was nothing passive about the way Courtney made love. She knew what she wanted and let him know. Not only that, she knew exactly how to push him to the brink and then pleasure him even more before finally sending him over the edge. He'd slept with a lot of women, and it might sound clichéd, but she'd rocked his world like no other woman ever had. He didn't know how long she planned to stay in Hawaii, but he hoped it was for at least several days, because one night with her would not be enough. Not by a long shot.

Is that the best of ideas? the annoying, responsible voice in his head once again asked him. It had spoken up during dinner as well and reminded him that this was his friend Trent's cousin. While Josh had numerous acquaintances, the list of people he considered friends was short, and he'd like to keep Trent on it. Sleeping with his buddy's cousin might make things between them awkward.

On the other hand, what were the odds he'd ever find out? The guy didn't spend his time reading tabloid magazines, and Josh sure as hell would never tell him. He didn't think Courtney would either. And if Trent found out, it might not bother him. After all, they were all consenting adults.

Courtney entered the room carrying a tray and put an end to his thoughts. "I wasn't sure what you'd like, so I got an assortment of things." After setting the tray on the nightstand, she handed him a glass of wine and sat down next to him.

Josh took a sip and considered his words. He wasn't looking for anything long-term. He'd tried that once, and it hadn't ended well. At the same time, he didn't want his time with Courtney to be just a one-night thing either.

"I'm not fussy." He glanced over at the assortment of foods. He didn't know how long she'd been there, but she had a well-stocked kitchen. Reaching around her, he grabbed a strawberry. "Do you have any plans for tomorrow?"

"My goal for the next two weeks is to just play it by ear."

She sipped her drink before setting it aside and adding grapes and cheese to a small plate.

He planned to stay for the next two weeks too before flying back to Maine and making sure everything was ready there before he picked up his four-year-old daughter, who'd be staying with him for a month. "Is that how long you're staying?"

Courtney nodded as she popped a grape in her mouth. "I want to be back in time for the election. My cousin is running for the Senate," she added once she swallowed.

He didn't bother with politics. In his opinion, the people in Washington were a lot like preschoolers all fighting to get their own way. However, even he'd heard about the upcoming election involving her cousin.

"A friend of mine keeps a sailboat here. I'm taking it out tomorrow." Josh touched her knee and then ran his fingers up her thigh and under the hem of her robe. He didn't stop until he reached the junction between her legs. He heard her sharp intake of breath and smiled as he teased her. "Do you want to join me?"

THREE

YOU'RE MEETING *with his brother. Josh won't be there.* For all she knew, Josh might not even be in New England at the moment. He might have taken his daughter, who was staying with him until the end of the month, to the theme parks in Florida or California. Despite knowing this, the butterflies in her stomach refused to disappear. She hadn't seen or talked to Josh since their last night together in Hawaii. Countless times though she'd pulled up his contact information, which was still stored in her phone, and considered calling him. But each time she reminded herself that Josh Williamson didn't do permanent relationships. And although there'd seemed to be more between them than pure physical enjoyment, it had probably been all one-sided, since he hadn't asked to see her once they returned to their real lives. The fact he'd never called her reinforced her assumption their time in Hawaii together had been nothing more than a fun way for him to pass some time.

"What's wrong?" Addie, her cousin Trent's wife, asked.

Since Courtney started her new position, they often had lunch together. Addie's interior design firm was located in the same building as the Helping Hands Foundation. Today they'd opted for Ambrosia, the pastry shop and café on Benefit Street owned by Addie's family.

Shaking her head, Courtney reached for her hot chocolate and not for the first time wished her family had settled someplace warm and tropical. When she woke up this morning, the weather app on her phone claimed it was ten degrees, but thanks to the windchill factor, it felt like negative two. Even now at one o'clock in the afternoon, the temperature only hovered around twenty-three, which was still a far cry from the seventy-seven degrees her weather app said Hawaii was experiencing today.

"Could've fooled me. I've asked you the same question twice now."

Had she? Honestly, Courtney didn't know. "Sorry, I zoned out there for a minute." If thinking about Josh and their time together could truly be classified as zoning out, she did it way more than she should. "What was your question?"

"I asked if you wanted to come by for dinner Saturday night. My brother Tom is going to be in town, and he's staying with us instead of with my mom and dad."

The youngest of the family, Addie had four older brothers, and sometimes Courtney wondered how she'd survived. She had just one, and growing up, Scott could be the most annoying person alive, but at least she'd had a sister to help her annoy Scott right back. She'd only met Tom once, and it had been at Addie's and Trent's wedding. From what she remembered, he looked a lot like his brother Rock, who was engaged to her cousin Allison, but had been a little more easygoing.

"At the moment I don't have any plans for the weekend."

"Excellent, then I'll see you Saturday night?"

Something's up. It wasn't Addie's words but her tone that

suggested she was planning something other than a nice family get-together. "Who else will be there?"

Suddenly the half-finished sandwich on Addie's plate became the most interesting thing in the world. "As of right now, just Trent, me, Kendrick, and Tom."

Since Kendrick was Addie and Trent's young son, he didn't count. "Are you playing matchmaker again?"

On two different occasions, Addie had played cupid, and in both instances, the couples had ended up engaged. If that was Addie's intention now, Courtney appreciated the thought, but she wasn't interested.

"No."

In Courtney's opinion, the denial came a little too quickly. "Really?"

"Fine, maybe a little. But I did also invite Gray and Kiera as well as Derek and Brooklyn. Derek and Brooklyn can't come; they already have plans. Gray's going to let me know by tomorrow."

Courtney truly enjoyed spending time with her cousin, his wife, and son. Countless times since her move back to Providence, she'd spent time at their place. She hated to deny herself another enjoyable evening with them. "I'll come as long as you promise not to force Tom and me together."

"Fair enough. It probably isn't a good idea anyway. Tom will only be in town for the week."

Addie appeared deep in thought as she reached for the other half of her sandwich, and Courtney simply couldn't resist. "Trying to decide on your next victim, Cupid?" she asked.

Shaking her head, Addie laughed. "No, just trying to decide if I should ask you something I promised myself I wouldn't."

Okay, a comment like that would get anyone's attention. "Go for it." It wasn't like she had any secrets.

"I was scrolling through the internet yesterday and came across an article about Josh Williamson. According to the article, he's been keeping a low profile for the past few weeks and no one has seen him with anyone since you."

Delight snuck its way into her chest. Since her return from Hawaii, she'd gone out of her way to avoid any sites that might mention Josh and who he was spending time with.

"And I wondered if that was because the two of you were together," Addie said.

She'd known going in that she'd be just another woman as far as Josh was concerned. Unfortunately, that didn't change the fact she wished the opposite was true. "Nope. We haven't talked since I was on vacation."

"You could always call him, Courtney."

She could, but she wouldn't. "Did I miss the memo that said I wanted to talk to him?"

"No." Addie drew out the word before continuing. "But I saw the pictures of you two together. I know you. Regardless of how good the sex was, you wouldn't have spent so much time with him if you didn't like him. Maybe your sister would have, but not you."

How did she respond to that? "We had fun together, but we're not compatible long-term. Besides, he's too much like Trent was before he met you. Even if I wanted a relationship with him, he wouldn't be interested."

"Key word there, my friend, is before Trent met me. Maybe you're the person Josh needs to settle down." Courtney opened her mouth, a rebuttal prepared, but Addie didn't give her a chance to speak. Instead, she held up her hands and continued. "I promise not to bring up the subject again, but think about what I said."

Addie's words bounced around in her head throughout the rest of their lunch. Even as she prepared what she needed for her meeting with Evan Williamson, Josh's older brother, they haunted her. Trent had been like Josh in almost every way. It had taken meeting the right person for him to change and settle down. The same might be true of Josh—not that Courtney believed she was the one for him, but they did have a lot in common, and they'd had a lot of fun together both in and out of the bedroom. Maybe she should call him and just see what happened.

Later, when she wasn't about to head off to a meeting with his brother, she'd give it more thought. Right now she had her meeting at Epic Gaming to focus on.

Rather than have his assistant call and set things up, Evan had called himself. He claimed he wanted to partner up with the foundation and help with its charity programs. She'd agreed to the meeting immediately, even though the idea of sitting across from Josh's brother unnerved her a bit. The chances of Evan not knowing about her little fling with his younger brother were virtually nonexistent.

JOSH LISTENED to his attorney and once again wondered what the hell his ex-girlfriend, Naomi, was thinking. For the past three and half years, they'd shared custody of their daughter without any problems. They even made an effort to spend the major holidays and Adalynn's birthday together whenever possible so she could celebrate with both of them. Well, they had until Naomi moved in with her fiancé. Still, not once in all that time had Naomi suggested she would file for sole custody someday. Yet, she'd done just that right before he arrived home from Hawaii last month. So rather than arriving home and spending a few days making sure everything was ready for Adalynn's visit before picking his daughter up the day after Christmas, he arrived home to a letter listing the date and time to report to the courthouse. Unfortunately Judge Dennis

Wilkins, who'd heard their case, had a known track record of always ruling in the mother's favor regardless of the facts. Between that and the fact Naomi's lawyer claimed things that were not true, it hadn't surprised him when the judge awarded Naomi temporary sole custody until either their next court date or, as Josh hoped, Naomi changed her mind, because the last thing he wanted was the media to learn about this. If they did, they'd drag his daughter into the limelight. Unfortunately, that had been weeks ago, and so far, Naomi hadn't dropped her suit.

"If anything changes, I'll be in touch," David Kensington, Josh's attorney, said.

"Thanks." Ending the call, Josh resisted the urge to hurl the cell phone across the room and instead placed it down on the conference table.

"Any new updates?" Evan, his older brother, asked.

At the moment, they, along with Pauline Carten, Josh's publicist, were seated inside Evan's downtown Providence office. While Josh had taken after their mother and her love of acting, Evan had inherited their father's entrepreneurial spirit. His most recent endeavor was a video and computer game company. It, like all of Evan's previous endeavors, was doing phenomenally well.

Shaking his head, Josh reached for his coffee, but rather than take a sip, he set the cup back down. Right now his stomach was so much of a mess, he wasn't sure adding anything to it was a good idea. "Just more of the same."

Frequently movie roles forced him to pretend to be in love with a woman. He regularly kissed costars and appeared in intimate situations with them while the cameras rolled. It never caused him sleepless nights or upset stomachs, because it was his job. What they planned to propose in this meeting was something else entirely, and he'd been having second and third thoughts about it all week.

Courtney's perfect for the role. For at least the tenth time since he agreed to the plan, he reminded himself of this fact. Her reputation was without a single blemish, and the media had already circulated several pictures of them together in Hawaii, making it easier for them to pull off the charade. Perfect or not, his conscience kept jabbing him, urging him to rethink the plan.

They'd been almost inseparable while in Hawaii. While they'd spent every night together in either her suite or his, they'd spent their days outside doing everything from surfing and sailing to lounging by the pool. And for the first time in longer than he cared to admit, he'd felt connected to a woman. He'd not only enjoyed making love to her, but he'd enjoyed talking and spending time with her. Despite their different personalities, they had a lot in common. When he'd left her suite his final night in Hawaii, he'd considered asking if she wanted to continue their relationship once they returned home. He'd kept his mouth shut though, because she'd said nothing to make him think their time together was anything more than a fun fling while on vacation.

"Relax. Everything will work out," Pauline said. The plan they were about to propose was her idea.

Relax. Yeah, it was easy for Pauline to say that. She wasn't the one in danger of having only visitation rights.

"I'm confident she'll agree. But if she doesn't, I have a backup in mind," his publicist continued.

Leave it to Pauline to always have multiple strategies prepared. It was just one of the reasons she was at the top of her profession.

Unless Courtney refused, who the backup was didn't matter. Regardless, he wanted to know. "Who?"

"My cousin. Kym graduated from Juilliard. She's done a few commercials and some small parts on television but so far has had no luck landing any big roles. A marriage to you would help her career immensely. And she knows how to keep a secret. But I really don't think I'll need to get her involved." Pauline patted his hand in an almost motherly fashion.

Actually, in a lot of ways she acted more like a mother than his mom, Scarlett, who'd more or less grown up in front of a movie camera. Before she'd met and married his father, she'd partied with the best of them. Her partying ways remained almost nonexistent until after Josh's younger sister was born and his mom went back to acting. It wasn't long after that his parents divorced, and his mom went on to spend her time with countless men before marrying and divorcing husband number two and then marrying her current husband, Trevor Basto, six years ago. Since Josh's life mirrored hers in so many ways, his mom never criticized him or told him to reconsider his behavior. On the other hand, his publicist, who oddly enough wasn't much older than him, thought nothing of doing both. And now he wished he'd listened to her a little more.

"I think there's a decent chance Courtney will agree. If she doesn't, we'll worry about it then," Evan said from across the table.

From the start, he'd agreed marriage to Courtney would crush much of the muscle behind Naomi's arguments, especially the fabricated ones for sole custody. He hoped it would also convince her to drop the suit entirely, because if they went to court, the media would be all over it, which meant Adalynn would be dragged through the tabloids too. And he'd do anything to keep her protected.

A knock on the office door prevented Josh from replying, and a moment later Robin, Evan's personal assistant, stepped inside.

"Evan, Ms. Belmont is here," she said.

Regardless of whether it was Evan's personal assistant or someone on the janitorial staff, all the employees at Epic Gaming called his brother by his given name. According to

Evan, he wanted everyone at the company to feel like an equal. While Josh approved of his brother's sentiments, their dad didn't. He believed no one outside of upper management should call the CEO by his first name. In true Evan fashion though, he'd told their father what he could do with his antiquated beliefs.

"Thanks, Robin." Evan stood and followed his assistant out.

When the door opened a moment later, Evan reentered the room with Courtney a step or two behind him, and Josh's heart missed a beat. Until now, he hadn't realized how much he'd missed her. With her only feet away, he recognized what an ass he'd been not to reach out to her since leaving her hotel suite.

"You already know my brother, Josh. And this is his publicist, Pauline Carten." Evan gestured toward Pauline.

Courtney didn't immediately reply or even move. Instead, she stared at him and then blinked a few times, as if she didn't believe what she was seeing. After the third time, she stepped closer to the table and extended her hand in Pauline's direction. "Courtney Belmont. It's nice to meet you." Rather than select a seat, she glanced at him and nodded. "Josh, I um.... I didn't know you would be here today. It's nice to see you again. Have you been in Providence long?"

He wasn't sure what he'd expected her to show up wearing, but it wasn't the navy blue pinstripe wool skirt and matching blazer. In Hawaii she'd always worn colorful outfits, and somehow the dark business suit reminded him how much he still didn't know about her.

"About a week. How have you been?"

"A little busy but otherwise fine. You?"

He would have preferred to continue their polite but friendly conversation rather than get to the real reason for the meeting, but Evan had other ideas.

"Please make yourself comfortable. Can I get you anything, Courtney?" Evan pulled out a chair for her at about the same time Josh lost the battle to do the same thing himself. If he'd pulled out the chair, it would have been the one next to him, not the one across the table.

"I'm fine for now, thank you." Her eyes never strayed from him as she replied and sat down.

With everyone seated and the pleasantries out of the way, Evan didn't waste any time getting down to business. "Before we get started, I want to apologize for not being upfront about today's meeting."

Her forehead wrinkled in confusion, but much to Josh's relief she didn't get up and leave, something he'd feared would happen once Evan came clean.

They'd discussed Josh meeting with Courtney alone, however Pauline insisted it was a better idea for her to come to Evan's office, eliminating the possibility any pictures of them would surface in case she refused to go along with their plan. At the time, Pauline's argument seemed reasonable. Now though, he wished he'd called Courtney and arranged a private meeting with her rather than have his appearance here blindside her.

"While I do have a proposal I want to discuss with you regarding Epic Gaming and the foundation, it isn't the only reason I arranged this meeting," Evan continued.

"Okay, and what is your other reason?" she asked in a tone filled with both suspicion and interest.

"I'm sure you're—" Evan began.

"One of the reasons we asked you here was to tell you Evan and I are each donating one million dollars to the foundation." Josh appreciated his brother's help, but Courtney deserved to hear the truth from him. "The second is because I'm hoping you'll be willing to help me."

· · ·

AFTER COURTNEY GOT over the shock of seeing Josh again, she wondered if she'd made a mistake and her meeting with Evan was tomorrow. As far as she knew, Josh had nothing to do with his brother's company, so there was no reason for him to be here. It took only a matter of seconds for her to dismiss her theory that she'd showed up at the wrong time or day. Evan's assistant would've told her the meeting was another day, not let Evan know she was here. Now that her initial shock at seeing Josh was gone, other emotions were taking over, most of them attached to the memories she had of their time together.

Focus. Later she could deal with her feelings and the images going through her head. For whatever reason, Josh hadn't contacted her directly, but at the same time he claimed he needed her help.

"You already know I have a daughter," he continued.

Thanks to Josh's efforts, pictures of his daughter rarely appeared in the media, but he'd showed her several photos while in Hawaii. There was no denying the family resemblance between the two of them.

Nodding, Courtney wondered where the conversation was headed.

"Since Adalynn's birth, her mother and I have shared joint custody. Last month while I was in Hawaii, Naomi filed for sole custody. If the courts grant it, I'll have almost no say in any aspect of her life and I'll only get weekend visits."

Unless the woman had an incredibly good reason, it sounded like a bitchy thing to do, especially after all this time.

"She claims my reputation and career make me an unfit father."

Josh sounded past the point of frustrated, and she could understand why. "Josh, I'm sorry you're dealing with this, but I'm not sure how I can help. I know nothing about family law."

"I can control what new projects I take on. At the moment, I have nothing planned, and if I have to give up acting to keep custody of Adalynn, I'll do it in a heartbeat. My reputation is another matter. I can't change the past. But..." Josh paused as if searching for the right words. "If I was married, it would go a long way to fixing it—especially if I'm married to you."

A dancing bear in a pink tutu could walk in the room right now and she wouldn't be any more surprised. "I must have missed something," she said before he continued. She didn't think she had, but a more appropriate response escaped her. "Are you asking me to marry you?"

Josh nodded.

Yep, this was by far turning into the most bizarre meeting she ever attended. "Putting aside all the other reasons this is a crazy idea, don't you think it'll appear odd if we suddenly get married? We spent all of two weeks together in December and haven't seen each other since."

"Josh hasn't been seen in the company of anyone but you since early June, before he went on location in New Zealand. It would be easy to spin a story that you kept your relationship a secret leading up to your trip in December. And only the four of us here know that today is the first time you've seen each other in weeks," Pauline said, joining the conversation for the first time.

If his publicist said he hadn't been with any other woman but her in months, she couldn't argue. If anyone in this room besides Josh would know, it would be her. It didn't change the fact what he was proposing was a crazy idea.

"I know I'm asking a lot," Josh said, cutting into her thoughts.

Talk about an understatement. "You think?" The words slipped out before she could stop them, because nutty idea or not, she needed to remain professional.

"We obviously don't have to stay married indefinitely."

If Josh was asking for any other favor from her, she'd tell him to sign her up. But this went as far beyond a favor as anyone could ask. At the same time, if she refused, would Josh and Evan withhold their donation? While they received some generous contributions from donors, they didn't get two million dollars every day.

"I'm not sure, Josh. I need time to think about it." Part of her, probably the part she should be ignoring, was telling her to go for it. They'd had a lot of fun together in Hawaii, and she had missed him the past few weeks. If she said no, she'd kill any chance she might have with him. Her logical side, the side she should listen to, was urging her to say "thank you for the offer, but I'm not interested."

Unfortunately, she was interested. Despite her repeated reminders not to get emotionally involved while they were together in Hawaii, she had. And seeing Josh again today had those emotions surging toward the surface again.

"Understandable," he said.

She'd expected an argument from him. After all, the sooner they got married, the better, considering the situation he'd explained. "I'll call you no later than Thursday." Perhaps thinking she'd have a decision anytime this decade was being optimistic, but she needed to tell him something.

"And just so you know, the donations are not contingent on your decision."

Thank goodness.

Pauline appeared ready to speak. Perhaps she thought they needed an answer sooner. Whatever the publicist intended to say, she didn't get the chance.

"Evan, now is probably a good time to discuss the proposal you have," Josh said, rather than pressure her for an immediate answer.

For the next forty minutes, Evan shared his ideas for how Epic could partner with the foundation. Courtney did her best to follow along, but her mind repeatedly drifted away from the portfolio Evan handed her and to the man across the table.

The man who wanted to marry her so he wouldn't lose joint custody of his little girl. It truly was the craziest request she'd ever received, but one she was tempted to agree to. Being married to Josh certainly wouldn't be the worst thing in the world.

"Before you leave, I want to make sure you know your answer to what we discussed earlier will not effect this partnership," Evan said once they finished reviewing the information he'd presented her with.

"I'll need sometime to review this in more detail. I'll be in touch soon about everything we discussed today." She reached for the briefcase she'd set on the floor. Her meeting with Evan wasn't her only one this afternoon. She had another one back at her office in an hour. She not only wanted but also needed some time alone to get her head back to where it needed to be before her appointment walked through the door.

After exchanging the appropriate goodbyes, she pushed in her chair and stepped toward the door. Before she could move any further, Josh stood and came around the table. "I'll walk with you."

Evidently, sorting her thoughts would have to wait another few minutes.

Neither of them spoke as they walked past Evan's personal assistant and the other offices located on the floor. Despite the lack of conversation, she remained very aware that he stood less than an arm's length away.

Josh waited until they were safely alone behind the elevator doors before facing her. "I've thought about calling you several times since last month."

Her heart did a little dance. He sounded sincere. Maybe she hadn't imagined the connection in Hawaii. Then again, it was possible he was trying to sway her decision.

"And not because of what we just discussed," he continued.

The man was an actor, so at least for the moment she would take everything he said with a grain of salt.

"I wanted to explain the situation to you in private, but Pauline thought it would be best if we met here instead. I shouldn't have listened to her though. I'm sorry."

Whether he'd asked for her help in the privacy of her apartment or in his brother's office wouldn't have changed much. "It would have been an awkward conversation regardless, Josh."

"You're probably right." He took a step closer, and her brain conjured up the memory of them embracing on her balcony while they watched the fireworks. "Are you busy tonight?" he asked.

Wednesday night she had book club. This month, her friend Meg, who also lived at the Mayfair, was hosting. Then on Thursday she tentatively had plans to get together with a college friend who might be in the area, but tonight her calendar was wide open. "No."

"I'd like a chance to catch up. I'm having dinner with my dad and stepmom around six, but we should be done by eight."

She wouldn't mind more than a chance to catch up. But indulging in more of the fun they'd shared in Hawaii would only complicate the decision she needed to make. "I'll be home if you want to stop by. I live at the Mayfair in the penthouse. I'll let the doorman know I'm expecting you so he'll let you in."

When she first started looking for a place to live in Providence, she'd considered the Hillcrest, the city's premier condo building. As gorgeous as the building was, the fact three of her cousins already called it home convinced her to look elsewhere. She loved her family, but she didn't want someone checking up on her. Considering how protective Trent, Gray, and Derek could be when it came to the female members of the family, exactly that would've happened. While the Mayfair wasn't as new as the Hillcrest, she'd fallen in love with the building's penthouse apartment the moment she stepped inside.

The elevator doors opened, and they stepped out together. She expected him to stop, but he kept walking alongside her toward the entrance to the building's parking garage.

"I'll be over after dinner. Do you want me to call you first?"

A blast of cold air hit her head-on when they stepped outside, and she shivered. "No need, unless your plans change and you decide not to come."

His index finger moved across her hand, and she shivered again, although this time it had nothing to do with the cold temperature. "Won't happen. I'll see you later."

FOUR

No question about it, Josh had more in common with his mom than his dad, but he always preferred spending time with his dad and stepmom, Laura. Throughout their meal tonight though, he kept looking at his watch and wondering when the evening would end. While his dad and stepmom knew about the custody issues, they both assumed he planned to leave the situation in the hands of his capable, if expensive, attorney. Their assumption led to numerous questions and suggestions, none of which even came close to the plan he'd laid out to Courtney earlier—something he had no intention of telling them about. While they might understand the reasoning behind it, neither would approve. He didn't intend to share the plan with his mom either but for a different reason. Even if it was a matter of life and death, the woman couldn't keep a secret. If Courtney agreed to help him and his mom knew the real reason behind their marriage, the media and Naomi would eventually know too.

For the umpteenth time this evening, Josh checked the time. Almost seven thirty, and they were headed for the restaurant's exit. Not too bad. He'd guessed they'd leave the restaurant around eight.

"How much longer are you staying in the area?" his dad asked.

"I'm not sure." If things went the way he hoped, he'd be calling Providence home for the foreseeable future. As much as he'd rather have Courtney relocate to his house in Maine, he recognized her job was in the city. If she married him, he couldn't ask her to give up her position at the foundation.

"Laura and I are leaving on Friday. We'll be gone for most of the month. If you want to stay at the house instead of with Evan, you're more than welcome."

"Evan would miss me too much if I bailed on him now. But I appreciate the offer." Actually, it was the other way around. Most of the time he enjoyed the solitude of living alone, especially after months of working on a film, but since Naomi's bombshell, he'd found being alone only added to his despair. Being at Evan's this past week had helped.

Rather than get into the car the valet brought around, Laura hugged him. "If you get any updates while we're away, please call us." She might not be his biological mother, but she'd always treated him like a son and she viewed Adalynn as her granddaughter.

"I will." Depending on the answer he got from Courtney, he might be calling them for a very different reason within the next week or so.

Thanks to the time and the fact it was a Monday night, he didn't have to deal with a lot of traffic, which meant less than ten minutes after leaving Mon Soleil, his stepmom's favorite restaurant in the city, he pulled into the Mayfair's parking garage. Originally a hotel built at the turn of the twentieth century, real estate developers had purchased the building fifteen years ago and turned it into what had been Providence's most luxurious condo complex until the Hillcrest, where his brother lived, was built.

Josh expected the first floor of the Mayfair to resemble the many other exclusive condo buildings he'd visited. Instead, he discovered that the developers had left at least this level relatively untouched. A grand central staircase went up to the second floor, and an enormous chandelier hung from an intricately carved ceiling. Even the glass elevator that the hotel had been well known for remained, and he watched for a moment as it traveled up. Thankfully, it wasn't the only one in the building, and he headed for the one closest to him.

He spotted the woman walking toward the elevator as the doors were closing. It wasn't until after he pressed the button to hold them open that he realized doing so might not have been the smartest of moves. If the woman lived in the building, there was a decent chance she knew who lived in the penthouse. Until Courtney made up her mind, it would be best if no one could put them in the same place together.

"Thank you," the woman said, stepping inside and selecting her floor. She moved to the opposite side of the elevator, but her eyes remained focused in his direction before briefly glancing at the control panel, which had only two floors lit up: hers and Courtney's. "You're J.T. Williamson. I was just watching *Over The Edge* last night. It's my favorite of your movies." She extended her hand toward him. "My name is Lexie."

"Nice to meet you."

"I hate to ask, but would you mind taking a picture with me? My friends will never believe I met you without proof."

He was known for never refusing to give an autograph or pose for a photo. He didn't want to start doing so now.

They managed two photos before the elevator stopped at the fifteenth floor and the doors opened to a thankfully deserted hallway. "Thanks again," Lexie said, stepping out.

Josh made the rest of the trip alone. Unlike the first time the elevator stopped, the doors didn't open to reveal a carpeted hallway. Instead, he stepped out into a small marble-tiled foyer several feet from a mahogany door. Oil paintings hung on the walls, and a chandelier much smaller than the one downstairs hung from the decorative ceiling, illuminating the area.

Unwelcome anxiety settled in his stomach as he pressed the doorbell. The anxiety changed into something he couldn't label though when Courtney opened the door. At some point since their meeting, she'd ditched her dark suit for white leggings and an oversized crimson sweater. She'd let her hair down as well, and he could almost feel it slipping through his fingers or across his bare chest.

"Hey." Courtney's greeting stopped him from calling up all the times and places her hair had come in contact with his skin. "Come on in." She stepped back so he could enter, and before she could change her mind and shut the door in his face, he crossed the threshold.

Whatever you do, don't kiss her. Maybe if he repeated the words enough times while he was here, he'd manage to keep himself from doing it. However, if he were a betting person, he'd say the odds weren't in his favor tonight.

He walked past her, and the barest hint of jasmine teased him. At least he thought he smelled it. In Hawaii, her hair had often smelled like jasmine, so it was possible he was imagining the scent now.

Other than to close the door, she didn't move. "I was about to pour myself coffee, would you like some?"

How long she'd let him stick around tonight was anyone's guess, but if she was offering him coffee, she intended to at least let him stay for more than five minutes.

"Sounds good."

He caught another whiff of jasmine when she passed by him, and the memory of Courtney resting her head on his shoulder while they sat on her balcony formed. They'd done it countless times during their two weeks together, sometimes talking about whatever came to mind and other times simply enjoying the view. His eyes dropped to her feet as he followed her. It didn't surprise him that she was barefoot. On vacation, she'd left her shoes and sandals behind whenever possible.

"Did you have dinner in the city?" Courtney entered the kitchen and removed two coffee mugs from a cabinet. Unlike his brother's kitchen, which consisted of sharp angles, black cabinets, and a lot of chrome, this one incorporated dark woods, granite, and an inverted ceiling that echoed back to the grand hotel the building had once been.

"We went to Mon Soleil. Laura loves it there." He'd meet Laura at the age of ten, and even though she treated him like a son, he'd never called her "Mom."

Picking up the French press coffeepot, she poured coffee into the mugs. "That's possibly my favorite restaurant in Providence." Courtney added cream and sugar to her drink, then took a sip, but her eyes never looked away from him as he fixed his coffee. "Unless you visit Paris, you won't find better French cuisine." Rather than set down her mug, she gestured toward the doorway with it. "We'll be more comfortable in the living room."

Josh took that as another good sign she didn't intend to kick him out anytime soon.

A unique combination of wood, leather, and various shades of red filled the living room. A door in the left-hand corner led out onto a balcony that wrapped around the corner of the building. Tonight it would be far too cold to sit out there, but in the spring and summer it would be a fabulous spot to sit and enjoy breakfast or dinner. Floor-to-ceiling windows provided an excellent view of the city, and during the day they would allow natural light to fill the room.

"This afternoon when you said you'd thought about calling

me several times, I wasn't sure I believed you." She opted to sit on the sofa and set her coffee down on the end table.

On his way over, he'd run through various conversation starters. He'd settled on asking her about how her new job was going. Evidently, she had ideas of her own, and he was fine with that.

"Honestly, Josh, I'm still not sure I do," she added with a slight shrug.

Considering the favor he'd asked her prior to telling her that, he understood her reluctance. "I—"

"But if you were being honest, I guess I should be too." She sounded conflicted about whatever she intended to tell him. "A few times, I pulled up your number and almost called you."

Despite the many places to sit, he dropped down onto the sofa with her. It might not be the wisest of decisions, since the urge to kiss her was growing stronger the longer he was with her, but it wouldn't be the first time he'd done something stupid. And it probably wouldn't be the last.

"I wish you had. I've missed you." Perhaps he should keep the truth to himself, since she might assume he was simply trying to convince her to do what he wanted. But he didn't want to. He wanted—no, he *needed* her to know the truth.

JOSH'S WORDS were just what she wanted to hear. Despite all the warnings she'd issued before he showed up, reminding herself to be cautious, a sliver of delight erupted in the vicinity of her chest.

He wants my help. Don't forget that.

She didn't want to believe it, but it was possible he'd say or do anything to get her to go along with his marriage proposal—a plan she'd been thinking about constantly since leaving his brother's office. No doubt about it, the entire idea was crazy. Unfortunately, the absurdity of the plan wasn't stopping her from seriously considering going along with it. She could honestly say she cared about Josh, and given time, she could see her feelings growing into much more.

Josh's request for help wasn't the only thing she'd thought about since the meeting this afternoon. She'd also spent more than a few minutes replaying their two weeks in Hawaii. While it was possible she was wrong, everything about their time together hinted that there had been more between them than sex. His words just further strengthened her belief.

"You had my number, Josh. You could have called me." Courtney knew full well what had stopped her from reaching out. She wanted to know his excuse.

With his coffee mug almost to his lips, he lowered it and nodded. "Yeah, I know. Like I said earlier, I thought about it. But the last time we saw each other, you didn't say anything about wanting to stay in contact. And this custody mess with Naomi...." Josh stopped and raked his hand through his hair. "I haven't been myself since I found out what Naomi was doing."

She could only imagine what he was going through. His daughter had come up more than once. While Josh might have the reputation of a carefree playboy, when it came to Adalynn, he seemed like a loving father who would do anything for his daughter. And he was right about her not bringing up the topic of staying in contact. Of course she had kept her mouth shut because of his well-known relationship history.

"Fair enough," Courtney admitted.

Again Josh raised his coffee mug toward his mouth. Like before, it didn't reach its final destination. "Why didn't you call?"

Did he really need to ask? She thought the answer would be obvious. "You don't exactly have a great track record when it comes to relationships, Josh. You're known to sleep with two different women in the same weekend. That's not the kind of behavior that suggests you'd be interested in something serious."

A muscle in his jaw clenched.

"You're right, I haven't been in a serious relationship since Naomi. But I've never slept with two different women in the same weekend. Gone out with two, sure, but that's it. Yeah, I know the media claims I have, but you know how good the media is at twisting the truth."

Countless times she'd seen how reporters made up stories or changed facts when writing pieces about her family. The same could very well be true in Josh's case. She wanted to believe it was, and for now she'd give him the benefit of the doubt.

She watched as the mug finally touched his lips, and he took a sip. What would he do if she removed it from his hands and settled her lips on his? She'd stopped herself from doing it when she opened the door tonight, but it had taken considerable willpower.

Start talking again.

If she kept her mouth busy talking, maybe she'd keep herself from kissing him. And kissing him before she had answers to her questions would be a bad idea. No, correction, it wouldn't be a bad idea, it would be a colossally bad one, because once they started kissing, she might give in and agree to anything.

Clearing her throat, she reached for her coffee and forced her gaze back to his eyes. "I've been thinking a lot about our meeting this afternoon."

"You don't have to give me an answer tonight. I didn't ask to see you because I expected one."

"I know, but the sooner I give you one the better. And I can't do that until I have a few questions answered." Another woman might drag her feet and make Josh jump through hoops before giving him an answer. She had no intention of doing either.

"Ask me whatever you want." Josh rested his ankle on his knee and draped an arm along the back of the sofa.

"How soon would you want to get married?"

"Within a couple of weeks. I thought we could tell people we got engaged while in Hawaii."

Yeah, she'd expected as much. Then again, she wouldn't be the first person in her family to have an exceptionally short engagement. "Where would we live? I can't move to Maine."

While she could do some work remotely, she needed to remain within commuting distance of the foundation. As far as she knew, the only house he had in New England was in Bar Harbor, a town more than five hours away, making a daily commute impossible.

"I've already considered that. We can either buy some-thing in the area or I can move in here. Whatever you want. It doesn't matter to me."

"I'd rather stay here." She'd moved in the middle of November and had no desire to do it again. Besides, it wasn't like she didn't have more than enough room here for two people. "We'll need to have a prenup." If she'd been entering into a marriage like her brother's, she wouldn't consider it. But this wouldn't be anything like what her brother and Paige had. She needed to know that when it ended, she would be protected.

"Not a problem." Josh picked up his coffee and took another sip. Once again, she wished his lips were touching her rather than the mug.

Looking away from his mouth, Courtney focused on a painting hanging on the far wall and sipped her coffee. So far, he'd given her all the right answers. But she had one more question she needed answered. If she was being honest with herself, she wasn't sure how she wanted him to answer when it came to this one.

She'd slept with the man, so asking him if he expected them to be intimate shouldn't bother her. Yet it did. Tightening her grip on the mug, she asked her final question. "How real of a marriage do you expect this to be?"

Setting aside his coffee, he slid closer to her. "When we're in public, it has to appear 100 percent real. Except for Evan, not even our families can know the truth." His hand closed around her shoulder as his thumb caressed the skin along the neckline of her sweater. Each pass sent another spark to the tiny fire growing insider her. "But when it's just the two of us here, it'll be up to you."

She'd have to put some thought into whether or not they'd be intimate, because on one hand, sleeping with him while they were married might not be the wisest of moves. At the same time though, if she agreed to this, she might as well be able to enjoy the perks. Correction, not if, but *when* she agreed. It might turn into an epic disaster, but she intended to help him. Even before he walked in, she'd been leaning in that direction. The only thing holding her back had been the need for answers to her questions, which she now had.

"Do you—"

"I'll do it," Courtney said at the same time.

His whole face spread into a smile, and he cupped the back of her head before brushing his lips against hers. The feel of his mouth against hers again caused the fire inside her to go from a small and manageable one to an out-of-control wildfire. Before she could fully enjoy it though, he pulled away, his face a mask of seriousness.

"Are you positive?" Josh asked, his tone both cautious and optimistic. "You usually stay out of the media. If we do this, you won't be able to do that. The tabloids will be all over us, Courtney. Not everyone can handle it."

The last part of his statement had her wondering if the media had played a role in the ending of his relationship with Naomi. Other than to tell her Naomi was the mother of his daughter, Josh hadn't given her any details about their one-time relationship.

"Trust me, I already considered that. I'll be fine. It's not like the media has never bothered me before."

Josh's smile returned, and the hand on her shoulder slipped down to her waist. "Thank you."

He brought his mouth down on hers and pulled her in closer. Memories of him holding her close once again bombarded her, and she briefly considered inviting him to stay the night. Common sense kicked in before she could do something she might later regret. Before she allowed their relationship to become intimate again, she needed to know for certain it was what she wanted. Courtney couldn't make a decision like that with his lips and body touching hers.

Ending their kiss, she moved her hand, which had found its way to the back of his neck, and put some much needed space between them. "We should talk about how we're going to proceed." She wrapped both hands around her coffee mug again. She couldn't touch Josh if they were both occupied.

"If you agreed, Evan said he'd pick up an engagement ring for me. Since we're going to claim I proposed weeks ago, it'll be safer if I'm not seen by anyone shopping for a diamond ring."

A twinge of disappointment bubbled up at the thought of another man buying the ring. But she couldn't argue with his reasoning. It would look odd if anyone ever found out he'd bought the ring a day or two before they went public with their relationship.

"I'll ask him to do it tomorrow. What size ring do you wear?"

Courtney didn't shop for clothes or purses as much as some women, but she had a weakness when it came to jewelry, especially rings. Since there was no written rule stating an engagement ring had to be a diamond, she had the perfect piece to fulfill the role.

"Don't worry about it. I have something I can use."

The ten-carat oval ruby surrounded by fourteen solitaire diamonds had caught her eye the previous winter during a shopping trip in Manhattan. With so many options in her collection, she didn't wear any one piece often, so no one in her family would remember seeing it on her prior to their announcement.

"Are you sure?"

"Positive. Besides, this way I can start wearing it tomorrow. If Evan purchases something, it'll need to be sized to fit me, which won't fit with the narrative that you proposed last month."

"Okay. I'll ask Pauline to prepare an announcement for the media outlets. Knowing her though, she already has one done."

"You were confident I would agree." She wasn't sure how she felt about that.

"She was. Honestly, I didn't know how you'd react."

"In the meantime, we should both contact lawyers regarding a prenup." She didn't have a lawyer per se, but her cousin Derek worked in one of the largest firms in the city. He should be able to either help her out or get her in contact with someone who could. "We don't have much time to plan. If you want, I can ask my uncle Mark to marry us. He did it for Derek and Brooklyn last year." Sometimes having an uncle who was a Rhode Island Supreme Court Chief Justice came in handy.

"Whatever you want is fine."

What she wanted and what they needed were not the same thing, but Josh didn't need to know that. "I'll talk to him tomorrow." She added calling her uncle to the mental to-do list forming. "I'll let my parents know too. Don't have Pauline release anything until after I have told them."

If her mom found out about the engagement from a social media post rather than from Courtney, it would devastate her. As it was, she was going to be disappointed she wouldn't be able to help Courtney plan a big, elaborate wedding similar to her cousin's the previous summer.

Josh nodded and picked up his coffee as she ran through their plan for any other holes or possible complications. "It's up to you, but it might help sell this whole thing if you move in here before news of our engagement goes public."

He drained the coffee left in his mug before he answered. "Yeah, I was thinking the same thing. I don't have a lot with me. I've been staying with Evan all week. I'll have to go up to Maine and get more clothes."

"Or we can go together this weekend. Either way, tomorrow bring what you have at Evan's here." She'd never been to Bar Harbor, but she'd heard it was a beautiful seaside town. A short getaway up there could make for an enjoyable weekend. "Do you have any plans for Saturday?"

With everything else today until she mentioned the weekend, she'd forgotten about her conversation with Addie over lunch. She'd agreed to join Addie, Trent, and Addie's brother for dinner. If the world was going to learn she and Josh were engaged this week, she better show up Saturday night with him by her side or not go at all.

"No."

You do now. "I'm supposed to have dinner at Trent and Addie's. There is no way I can show up alone once news of our engagement goes public. You'll have to come with me."

Since Addie knew about her little fling with Josh last month, she assumed Trent knew as well even though, much to her relief, he hadn't mentioned it to her. She didn't know if

Trent had reached out and discussed it with Josh, but if he had, Addie hadn't shared the information.

"It'll be nice to see them. I haven't talked to Trent in months."

Courtney added letting her cousin's wife know to expect one more on Saturday as well as coming up with a good story to explain why she didn't tell Addie she was still with Josh this afternoon to her growing to-do list.

"We can't wait too long to make our engagement public." Josh interrupted the various storylines running through her head that would explain why she had lied to Addie. "Any idea of when Pauline can release a formal statement to the media?"

She wasn't looking forward to the conversation, but the sooner she told her parents they were engaged the better, especially since, as of tomorrow, people would see Josh entering and exiting the Mayfair.

"Let's plan on Wednesday. I'll tell my mom tomorrow, and she can let my dad know." She'd call her sister and brother as well. Whether she'd get a hold of either of them before they read about it somewhere was anyone's guess. "Are you going to tell your family beforehand?"

Other than his brother, Evan, she'd met no one in his family and knew little about them. Josh might not care how his parents learned of his upcoming marriage.

"In the morning, I'll give Dad and Laura a call. I have no idea where my mom is and getting a hold of her can be hard. If she doesn't hear about it from me, she'll learn about it like everyone else."

He sounded rather indifferent to the idea his mom might read about their engagement on a social media site, and she wondered what kind of relationship the two of them had.

"We should decide on exactly when and how we met," Josh said.

"Your publicist said no one has seen you with another

woman since before you left for New Zealand. When exactly did you travel there?"

Rather than pull the information from memory, he took out his cell phone and opened the calendar on it. "I flew out of Los Angeles on June 28 and stayed there until July 18. Then I spent about a month and a half on location in New York before heading down to Louisiana."

"How long did you stay there?" If this was going to work, they needed to get everything straight.

"Only two weeks before heading back to L.A. I remained there working until I flew out to Hawaii."

"It'll work best, I think, if we tell everyone we met while you were in New York. It's not unusual for me to head into Manhattan for a weekend, so I know my family will accept it. And if we do that, it'll appear as though we'd been together for almost five months before you proposed in December."

Five months wasn't a long time to be in a relationship before getting engaged, but she'd heard of shorter ones. And it was far better than telling everyone they'd spent all of two weeks together before getting engaged.

"Whatever you want. Any ideas about the how we met?"

Considering how much he had a stake, she would have thought he'd come up with a whole backstory long before their meeting earlier. "It might be easiest if we say we were both staying at the same hotel and met by the pool. It's at least some-what close to the truth."

"When I call Pauline, I give her the details so she knows how to answer any questions that come up."

Stifling a yawn, she checked her watch, expecting it to be much later than it was. She rarely went to bed before eleven, so she shouldn't be tired. Perhaps it'd been the stress of the day or the fact she'd gotten up much earlier than normal. What-ever the reason, she was exhausted and wanted nothing more than to curl up in bed and fall asleep.

As if reading her mind, Josh stood. "It's getting late. I'm going to head back to Evan's. What time should I come by tomorrow?"

"Plan to meet me here around six." Courtney added getting a key for Josh and making sure a guest room was ready to her mental list as she walked him to the door. As tempting as she might find him, at least for the time being, they were not sharing a bed.

Her fingers wrapped around the doorknob, but Josh's hand came down over hers before she could turn it. His green eyes searched her face for a moment. "I... thank you." Stepping closer, he kissed her cheek. "See you tomorrow night."

FIVE

DESPITE THEIR DIFFERENT CAREER PATHS AND LIFESTYLE choices, when it came to food, Josh had a lot in common with his older brother. So after selecting a box of Lucky Charms, just one of the many sugary kinds of cereal intended for kids lining the kitchen cabinet shelf, he filled a bowl while listening to Pauline.

"Do you care who I share the news with first?" she asked.

When it came to entertainment news sites, they were all the same to him. "You decide. But it can't go out until tomorrow." Opening the milk, he drowned his cereal before adding some to his coffee. "Courtney wants a chance to tell her family first."

"Did you decide on a wedding date?"

"No, but it'll be soon. When we decide, I'll let you know." If it was up to him, they'd get married this weekend, but he wasn't going to suggest that. She'd agreed to help him, so the least he could do was let her determine the where and when of their wedding.

"Okay. Keep me informed. Talk to you later."

Josh set aside his cell phone and managed to get a spoonful

of cereal in his mouth before his brother walked into the kitchen. When he'd arrived back at Evan's last night, his brother was still out.

Although Evan was dressed in a suit and tie, he grabbed the Lucky Charms still on the counter and poured himself a bowl. "How did it go last night?"

When he'd shared that he planned to visit Courtney last night, Evan advised against it. He thought she might feel pressured into helping Josh, thus hurting the chances she'd go along with their plan.

"Will you be my best man?" Like all brothers, they disagreed from time to time, but there wasn't anyone else he'd want standing next to him when he got married.

Evan pulled out one of the barstools around the kitchen island and sat. "She agreed?"

"Yesterday, weren't you claiming you were confident she would?"

"Yeah, but after she asked for some time to think about it, I thought it would be a few days before she gave you an answer." Evan ate a spoonful of cereal, then washed it down with some coffee.

"Me too, but I'm not complaining." Josh followed his brother's lead and reached for his spoon.

"I'll pick out a ring today."

"No need. She has that covered. And tonight I'm moving in with her."

Although he'd assumed they'd live in or around Providence after they got married, he hadn't expected Courtney to suggest he move in now. When she did though, he didn't need to think twice about his answer, and not because it would help sell their story. He wanted to once again be a part of her life in every way—or at least in every way she allowed. He'd understood her question last night perfectly well. She'd wanted to know if he expected them to have sex while married. While he sure as hell hoped so—the two weeks they'd been intimate had been like nothing else he'd experienced—he wasn't stupid enough to tell her that. Instead, he'd been upfront and let her know what he'd decided before even proposing the plan. Whether they continued their sexual relationship was up to her.

Leaving his seat, Evan popped two slices of bread in the toaster. "Want some?"

Some toast covered with strawberry jam sounded like the perfect companion for his cereal. "Yeah, sure."

"Did you already let Pauline know?" While his brother waited for the toast, he grabbed both the strawberry jam and the butter from the refrigerator.

With a mouthful of Lucky Charms, he nodded. "So will you be my best man?" He expected Evan to agree, but he'd never answered Josh's earlier question.

"Just tell me where and when," he answered.

The where he didn't care much about, but he'd like to know the when. Last night hadn't been the time to push for a specific date. She'd agreed it would be soon. He couldn't ask for much more than that.

For the next several minutes, their conversation switched to Evan's plans for the weekend. Since it was his girlfriend's birthday, he'd intended to take her to Valley's Edge, a ski resort on Stratton Mountain in Vermont. Prior to this week, Josh had never met Gemma, but from the way his brother talked about her, their relationship seemed serious.

"I'll make arrangements to donate the funds to the foundation," Evan said, adding his cereal bowl and plate to the dishwasher.

He'd taken care of getting the money to the foundation even before Courtney walked in his brother's office. And while Josh was sure she'd agreed to help partially because of the combined two million dollars they were donating to the foundation, he wanted to believe it wasn't the only reason.

Evan finished his coffee before putting the mug in the dishwasher as well. "Are you going to tell Mom and Dad or let them read about it like everyone else?"

Getting hold of their dad would be easy; their mom was another story. "I'll call them both later. For now, don't mention our engagement to anyone. Not even Gemma." He didn't want Evan's girlfriend finding out about his engagement and posting the news on some social media site before Courtney told her parents.

"Good luck with Dad."

Yeah, he already expected one of his dad's well-known lectures regarding some aspect of Josh's life his dad disagreed with. Usually, the lectures revolved around Josh's inability to commit to a woman and keep his name out of the tabloids. Occasionally, they involved the frivolous ways he spent money. There wasn't a doubt in his mind the fact he was going to marry a woman he'd known less than a year would set his dad off. At least in this instance, he didn't blame the man. If Josh had a son who planned to do what he was about to, he would share his opinion too.

Evan clapped him on the shoulder as he walked past him. "I won't tell anyone. Since you won't be here when I come home, call me if you need anything. And maybe next week the four of us can get together."

Josh polished off another bowl of cereal and two more slices of toast before following his brother's lead and adding his dirty dishes to the dishwasher. Then he grabbed his cell phone and pulled up his dad's number. The sooner he got the lecture out of the way the better.

COURTNEY HAD CLIMBED into bed as soon as Josh left. But rather than succumb to the exhaustion she'd felt while sitting on the sofa, she'd tossed and turned, her mind unwilling to turn off. After an hour of staring into the darkness, she'd thrown in the towel and switched on an old black-and-white sitcom. One had turned into another. Exactly at what point in the second one she'd fallen asleep, she wasn't sure. She knew when her alarm went off she had about as much energy as a rock and a cramp in her neck. A hot shower and coffee had helped with her energy problem; unfortunately, neither did a thing for her neck. The way she saw it though, the cramp was the least of her problems.

Setting down another cup of coffee, Courtney logged into her email as she again considered the best way to drop the news on her mom—just one of the many things that kept her up last night. It was either spend time thinking about her upcoming conversation or focus on Josh's answer to her question regarding how real he expected their marriage to be and the fact that in a matter of hours he'd be sleeping just down the hall. Like he'd done with all of her questions, he'd given her the perfect answer and promised the final decision was up to her.

Despite answering all her emails before leaving the office the previous night, a new batch required her attention now. Personally, she considered reading and responding to countless emails a major pain, which was why she always tried to tackle them as soon as she started her day. She much preferred to address issues and make plans either face-to-face or via a phone conversation. Considering the number of emails she got daily, she assumed she might be the only one though.

She got through the first five before her mind started wandering. Even though she'd given him the answer he wanted, he'd warned her about the media attention she'd face by being with him. Although it probably hadn't been his intention, the fact he'd given her a good reason not to agree with his plan told her something about him. He might be one of the biggest playboys in Hollywood and unable to commit to a woman for more than a few weeks, but he was honest. She'd rather be with an honest man who might be gone in a month than spend her life with one who lied and kept secrets.

"Focus." She was meeting with her mom in a little while. She needed to get as much done now as she could, because she didn't know how long she'd be in her mom's office. Considering what she needed to discuss, she might be in there for the rest of the day.

Six emails later, she pulled out the portfolio Evan had presented to her yesterday. At least on the surface, the partnership sounded like a win-win for the foundation as well as his company. Then again, she hadn't paid as much attention to the presentation as she should have—a fact that annoyed her because she prided herself on being not only professional at all times but competent and able to multitask. With Josh across the table from her, it had been all she could do to simply follow along rather than stare at the man.

Courtney hadn't gotten any further than the first page when someone knocked on her office door. The words "come in" were barely out of her mouth when the door opened and Addie entered. Occasionally, they'd meet for a late-morning coffee, but Addie always called to see if she was free; she never just showed up.

"What's the matter?" Various emergencies ran through Courtney's head that could explain Addie's unexpected visit. "Is Kendrick sick again?" A few weeks earlier, Addie and Trent's son had had bronchitis. She'd never seen anyone more miserable than the little boy.

Addie closed the door as she shook her head. "Kendrick's fine. I just wanted to talk to you before I leave to meet a client." She placed her coat on the back of a chair before sitting down.

With Addie sitting there, it would be as good a time as any to tell her about Josh joining them on Saturday night. Besides, running the story she'd come up with to explain her sudden engagement by Addie before she dropped it on her mom might not be a bad idea. It'd be like a trial run, allowing her to find any problems with it.

"Did you know Josh is in town?" Addie asked before Courtney could decide on the best way to begin.

Okay. How did Addie know Josh was in Providence? Last night he said he hadn't talked to Trent in months. Rather than answer the question, Courtney asked one, because she didn't want to believe he'd lied to her. "How do you know he's around?"

"Tracey..." Addie paused for a moment. "You remember Tracey, right?"

Courtney nodded. She'd met the nanny who took care of Kendrick during the day while Addie and Trent were at work, but she couldn't imagine how the woman would know Josh was in Rhode Island.

"When she arrived this morning, she mentioned it. She's a big fan of his and she regularly searches for any posts with the hashtag JTWilliamson. This morning a picture of him with a woman showed up. I don't remember the exact wording, but the caption said something like 'Look who I ran into at the Mayfair.' Tracey said the person tagged Providence as the location." Addie pulled her phone out of her purse and scrolled through the apps on the device before selecting one and handing the phone to Courtney.

A picture of Josh and a woman she'd never seen filled the screen. Sure enough, the caption attached to it read 'Look who I ran into at the Mayfair. JT Williamson!'

"Was he visiting you?" Judging by the tone of her voice,

Addie had already decided he had been.

Closing the app, Courtney handed the cell phone back. "Yes."

Addie's face lit up, and she smiled. "So you called him? Or did he call you?"

Here goes nothing. "Neither, actually."

A moment ago she'd been fine; now her mouth felt as if someone had filled it with cotton balls. Picking up her coffee, she took a gulp of the lukewarm liquid and grimaced. Coffee needed to be either hot or ice cold. Once it hit the stage in the middle, the best place for it was down the drain.

"Okay. That makes no sense at all. Care to explain?"

"Josh and I have been together for a while. Even before those pictures of us in Hawaii showed up."

If she didn't feel so guilty about lying, she would have laughed at Addie's stunned expression. "*Really?* Exactly how long is a while?" Addie asked.

"We met in July when he was in New York, and we've been together ever since." Good thing they'd discussed this last night, saving her from making it up as she went.

"July!" There was a decent chance Steven in the office next door had heard her. "Why didn't you tell me?"

She'd expected this question. "Since I wasn't sure how long it would last, I wanted to keep it out of the tabloids as long as possible. Keeping it a secret from everyone seemed like the safest route."

Across the desk, Addie frowned, and her shoulders slumped. "I wouldn't have told anyone." In the beginning of her and Trent's relationship, Addie had had her own run-in with the media, so she understood how relentless it could be.

"I wasn't worried you'd tell a reporter, but you might have let it slip to Trent. And I wasn't sure how he'd react, so until I knew there was something real between us, I didn't want him to know." She hadn't expected Addie to be upset because she hadn't confided in her. But at least to her, the excuse she'd pulled out of thin air sounded genuine.

"Then the two of you planned the vacation in Hawaii?"

Time to drop the rest of the surprise. Courtney twisted the ruby ring on her left hand and hoped Addie bought the rest of the story. "It was actually Josh's idea, but yes, we planned to meet there right after Scott's wedding. And while we were there, he proposed."

"Proposed?" Addie shifted in her seat and leaned an elbow on the desk. "As in asked you to marry him?" she asked, propping her chin up with her hand.

Courtney nodded and held out her left hand.

"You've been engaged since December?"

If Addie was having this much trouble accepting the news, what would happen when she told her mom?

"Congratulations, I guess." Confusion still tainted Addie's voice.

"I know most people would have shared the news long before now. We wanted to wait. You're the first person other than Josh's publicist to know."

"Then you don't want me to tell Trent?"

The fewer people she had to have this conversation with the better. "You can tell him. I'm meeting with my mom soon to tell her. Tomorrow, Pauline, Josh's publicist, is going to alert the media outlets."

Reaching for her hand, Addie examined the ring Courtney selected to act as an engagement ring. "He has good taste, anyway. Have you decided on a wedding date?"

"We don't want a long engagement. I'm going to ask Uncle Mark if he can perform the ceremony on February first."

She realized Josh would prefer something sooner, but unless they eloped, something her mom might disown her for doing, she needed some time to plan. And since they weren't going to have anything elaborate, a few weeks should be enough time—at least her cousin Derek and his wife had managed to pull off a nice wedding in a few weeks' time last year. Scott and Paige hadn't had a lot of time to plan either, and their wedding had gone off without any issues.

"That's only about a month away. I'm glad I'm not the one who has to tell your mom."

Courtney wished she wasn't either. "Since Josh is in town, I'm going to bring him with me on Saturday night. Is that okay?"

"Yeah, of course. And if you need any help with planning, I'm here for you." Addie stood and pulled on her coat. "See you this weekend."

Courtney watched her friend leave. Once the door closed behind her, she sagged back in her chair and blew out a breath. For the most part, the conversation had gone well. Although Addie was surprised, it didn't appear as if she doubted any part of the story. "Time for the second act," she muttered after a glance at her watch.

Angela, her mom's personal assistant, smiled when Courtney approached. A woman in her mid-sixties, she'd been with the foundation for as long as Courtney could remember.

"Mrs. Belmont said to have you go straight in," Angela said as she reached for the ringing phone on her desk.

Although she couldn't complain about her office, her mom's office was at least three times the size. In addition to a desk and a matching credenza, the room contained an oval-shaped conference table, a separate sitting area that her mom used for more relaxed meetings, as well as a private bathroom. Several pictures of Cooper, her only grandson at the moment, sat on the credenza. And no matter the time of year, there were always fresh flowers in the office. Today's arrangement consisted of white lilies, peach roses, carnations, and green echeveria succulent. It was anyone's guess what might be in the office next week.

"Hi, Courtney. I'll be right with you. I'm finishing up an email."

No need to rush.

Rather than sit near the desk, Courtney crossed the room and got comfortable on one of the two dove-gray sofas. As promised, Marilyn joined her almost immediately.

After sitting on the sofa across from Courtney, she put her cup down on the coffee table between them. "It seems like I haven't talked to you in ages."

While they both worked for the foundation these days and saw each other almost daily, it had been a while since they sat down and engaged in a conversation that didn't involve work.

"Have you talked to Scott?" her mom asked.

The next two people she planned to drop the news on were her brother and sister, but she hadn't wanted to reach out to them until after telling her mom. "Not recently."

"He called last night. Paige is having twins." Mom sounded as happy as a child who was about to get her first puppy.

She'd known Paige was pregnant. It had been the main reason for their short engagement. The idea her new sister-in-law might be expecting twins had never crossed her mind. While thrilled for the couple, she was glad it was Scott and Paige who were about to welcome twins into their lives and not her. She'd seen how much work Cooper could be, and he was just one child.

"They'll be here with Cooper for a few days," Marilyn added. "Assuming you and your sister aren't busy, I thought we could have a family get-together. I will call Juliette later. Do you have plans for the weekend?"

One never knew what Juliette might be up to. "I'm supposed to have dinner with Addie and Trent Saturday night."

"I know Paige and Scott plan to head home on Sunday,

so I'll see if your sister is available for brunch before they leave and get back to you. This morning you said you wanted to talk to me about something. What is it?" her mom asked.

Moistening her lips, Courtney prepared herself for whatever reaction she might receive. "I'm engaged. Actually, Josh and I have been since last month." Somehow saying the words was easier this time around.

"Engaged? Josh who? And why haven't your father and I met him?"

She'd assumed her mom never saw the pictures from Hawaii. Her statement seemed to confirm that fact. Either that, or Mom didn't know J.T. was a stage name.

The first answer was on the tip of her tongue, but before she could speak, Marilyn continued.

"Engaged since last month and you're only telling me now? I didn't even know you were dating anyone."

"We've been together since the summer. I wanted to keep our relationship out of the spotlight for as long as possible, so we didn't tell anyone. If I hadn't been sick on Christmas, I would have brought him by."

She'd woken up Christmas morning with her throat on fire and a fever of 102. It'd been the first Christmas she hadn't seen her parents. Still not 100 percent, she'd opted to skip the family's New Year's Eve party in Newport. At the time, she'd cursed her bad luck. Now, the fact she'd been sick helped sell the story.

"Do I know him?"

"You've met his brother, Evan Williamson. He participated in the bachelor auction. And you've probably seen Josh in movies. He goes by J.T. Williamson."

Recognition spread across Marilyn's face. "The *actor* from *Over The Edge*?"

Did she have to make the word actor sound so distasteful?

"Doesn't he have a reputation of being, well... you know, a player?"

They might be in a fake relationship, but she still felt the need to defend Josh. "We both know people can change, Mom. I know you love Trent, but even you have to admit his reputation was just as bad before he met Addie. Jake wasn't a saint either."

"You're right," her mom conceded, folding her hands in her lap. "Still, it would have been nice if your father and I met him before he proposed. Since your brother will be here, let us plan to get together this weekend even if your sister can't come so we can meet him."

She hated canceling on Addie, but the sooner she made the introduction and soothed her mom's hurt feelings the better. Courtney knew Addie would understand. "I'll reschedule with Addie and Trent. Josh and I will be by on Saturday night."

"Perfect. Hopefully, your sister can make it too." Mom picked up the coffee she'd carried over with her but hadn't touched since sitting down. "Have you discussed a wedding date? Personally, I think a summer or spring wedding would be better. Less chance of the weather causing problems."

And now came perhaps the worst part of the conversation. "February 1. I plan to ask Uncle Mark to perform the ceremony."

"Winter weddings can be beautiful too. Next February gives us more than a year to plan. And by then the election will be over, so it'll be more likely that Warren and Elizabeth can attend."

As much as she'd love her uncle Warren and aunt Elizabeth to be at the wedding, even if he wasn't in the middle of campaigning, the chances of him making it on such short notice were slim.

"We'll want to start looking for a dress soon. Do you think you'll have the wedding and reception at Cliff House?"

More than one of her cousins had used the family mansion, which currently belonged to her uncle Warren, in Newport for their weddings. Honestly though, she hadn't spent a single moment thinking about the where yet. She'd been far too busy concentrating on the conversation she was currently having. Tonight she'd bring up the matter with Josh.

"Mom, we're getting married this February, not next year."

The cup hit the table with a thud and some coffee sloshed over the side. "Are you pregnant?"

If she said yes, it might help her mom accept the short engagement. In a few months though, when it became obvious she wasn't expecting, she'd have a much bigger issue on her hands. "No."

"Then what's the rush? It takes at least six months to plan a decent wedding."

"Not true, and you know it. Derek and Brooklyn only had a few weeks to plan, and their wedding was perfect. Scott and Paige managed everything in less than six months." She checked each one off on her fingers. "Should I go on?"

Marilyn pressed her lips together and picked up her coffee again. "I still don't see the need to rush. At least wait until May or June."

"Mom, neither of us wants to wait, so unless Uncle Mark isn't available on the first, that's when we are getting married. I'd love your help with the planning."

With a sigh, her mom nodded. "I'll help in any way you need. But don't be surprised if your dad calls you later tonight and tries to change your mind about the date."

If he didn't, she would be surprised. But she had much bigger worries than a conversation with her dad, starting with the six-foot-one flesh-and-blood temptation that would be sleeping under the same roof as her starting tonight.

SIX

Josh's call to his dad after breakfast went straight to voice mail. The same thing happened when he tried his mom, although he'd expected as much in her case. The woman was impossible to get in touch with. While he left them both messages, they'd been vastly different ones. Considering the message he left his dad, Josh expected a call back before lunchtime. One never came though. Even now as he pulled into the garage at the Mayfair, he still hadn't heard from the man, and he wondered if he should try him again. Thanks to Pauline, news of his and Courtney's engagement would be front and center on multiple media sites tomorrow, including the ones associated with *Today Magazine* and the *Star Report*. He'd prefer if his dad and stepmom didn't find out he and Courtney were getting married from any of those. Oddly enough, he'd received a text message from his mom promising to call when she had a chance. In reality, that meant the call might come tonight or in another two weeks. It really was anyone's guess.

Popping the trunk, he removed his two suitcases. The cell phone in his back pocket went off as he settled them on the pavement. He slammed the trunk closed before pulling out the device.

"You couldn't have called an hour ago," he muttered when he saw *Dad* on the screen. "Hey, Dad." Rather than head into the warm building, he climbed back into his car. He'd prefer to keep this conversation private and, at the moment, inside his car was the only place he could guarantee he wouldn't be overheard.

"Sorry I didn't call you back sooner. This is the first chance I've had today. Did you get news from your lawyer?"

"No, what I want to talk to you about has nothing to do with Adalynn," Josh explained. "Before you hear about it from someone else, I wanted to tell you I'm engaged."

Silence followed Josh's statement, and he checked his watch while he waited for a response. Courtney had told him to come by around six. It was almost six now.

"This seems sudden. You didn't say anything about proposing to anyone when we saw you last night."

Across the parking garage, the stairwell door opened, and a couple stepped out. If they saw him and thought it odd that he was sitting in his car, they didn't show it. Instead, they walked past him and climbed into a vehicle further down the row.

"I asked Courtney back in December. At the time, we decided to wait to share the news."

More silence greeted his comment, and Josh got ready for a lecture.

"Congratulations, I guess," his dad finally said. "We won't have time this week, but when Laura and I get back, we'd love to meet her."

The fact his dad and stepmom were soon leaving for almost a month had completely slipped his mind. He'd prefer his dad be at the wedding, but he wasn't willing to postpone it to make it possible. "When are you getting back?"

"We're supposed to fly home on the twenty-ninth, but we might extend our vacation a few extra days."

"The wedding is on the first." He'd received the text message from Courtney after lunch letting him know her uncle would do the ceremony then.

More silence. Stewart Williamson was known for always having something to say. The fact he'd rendered his dad speechless so many times in one conversation demonstrated just how shocked his dad was by the news.

"I know patience isn't one of your strong points, but on this, I suggest you wait a few more months before getting married. How long have you even known this woman? Before now you've never mentioned her."

No way was he telling him the truth, and he didn't want to take the time to share the story they'd concocted. "Long enough, Dad. And we've already decided. Evan's agreed to be my best man, and I'm going to call Shannon later and tell her. Hopefully she can make it." His younger sister was finishing up a PhD program in Connecticut, so she might not have the time to come home.

"Listen, Dad, I need to go. I'll talk to you later." He didn't give his dad a chance to respond before disconnecting the call, because he was sure he'd get another comment about rethinking their wedding date. Stepping out of the car, Josh shoved the phone back in his pocket and hoped his dad didn't call back wanting to continue their conversation.

He picked up his pace when he saw a woman step inside the elevator at the other end of the lobby. She must have seen him approaching, because she held it for him.

Maneuvering his suitcases against the wall, Josh smiled. "Thanks."

"What floor are you going to?" Her finger hovered near the control panel where the button for the tenth floor was already lit up, but her eyes never strayed from his face.

"Penthouse, please."

Her eyes dropped down to the suitcases and then back to his face as she jabbed the button. "You look familiar, but I don't think I've ever seen you in the building before. Are you staying with friends?"

It wasn't any of this individual's business, but soon enough everyone would know anyway. Besides, answering her was better than being rude, and if he made one rude comment to anyone, the entire world might find out. "No, I'm moving in."

"Oh." The woman's mouth made a perfect O shape. "Well, welcome." She extended her hand. "My name is Meg."

Shaking her hand, he wondered how much longer until they reached the tenth floor. *Too Long.* "Nice to meet you."

"You look like J.T. Williamson," she said before he could give her his name. "I read he was in the building last night too. Was it you?"

Josh nodded, fully expecting Meg to ask for a picture like the woman from the night before. "Please call me Josh."

If Meg planned to ask for a photo, she didn't get the chance, because the doors opened, revealing a carpeted and thankfully empty hallway. "This is my floor. Have a nice night. I'm sure I'll see you around."

Before the doors closed again, he saw Meg pull a cell phone out of her purse. His instincts told him she was calling a friend to share she'd just met J.T. Williamson.

He had the elevator to himself for the rest of the ride. When he rang the doorbell, Courtney opened the door almost immediately, as if she'd known he was on his way up. With her phone against her ear, she gestured for him to enter but didn't stick around to make sure he did.

"Meg, I promise I'll call and explain everything tomorrow." Courtney's voice reached him as he shut the door. "I forgot that's tomorrow night," she said as she pulled out the sticks holding her hair up. He assumed they had a proper name, but to him, they resembled fancy chopsticks. "I might have to skip this month. I'll let you know." She dragged her hand through her hair. The innocent gesture conjured up all the times he'd done something similar while kissing her—an activity he'd love to engage in this evening.

After she ended the call, she set the device down on an end table and turned her attention on him. "That was my friend Meg. You just met her in the elevator. She was merely a little curious why I never told her you were moving in with me." A hint of frustration echoed in her voice.

So much for honesty being the best medicine. "Sorry. She asked if I was visiting when she saw the suitcases." If he'd known they were friends, he would have gone along with Meg's guess and let Courtney explain the truth when she got around to it.

"It's better that you ran into Meg rather than some of the other people who live in the building. She won't tell anyone tonight. Some of my neighbors would be posting it all over Twitter right now." Courtney gestured to his two suitcases. "Is that all you have?"

"Yeah. I packed light for this visit."

"I have three guest rooms. You can pick the one you want, but the one down the hall from me is the largest."

After her question last night about how real of a marriage he expected this to be, he'd known it was a long shot, but he'd hoped they'd pick up where they left off in Hawaii. If she was sticking him in a guest bedroom, that would not happen. At least not right away. If she was completely indifferent to him, she wouldn't have responded to his kiss the way she had yesterday. Instead, she would have pulled away and told him not to do it again.

"Put me wherever you want." This was still her place, and she was doing him the favor. The least he could do was play by her rules.

"Take the biggest one." She grabbed the handle of a suitcase and pulled it behind her.

As he followed her through the living room and down the hall, his eyes were more interested in checking her out rather than the place he'd be calling home for the foreseeable future. Tonight she was wearing a dark gray skirt that fell just below the knee, hiding the legs he remembered being wrapped around his waist while they made love. She'd paired the skirt with a silky-looking top the same shade of purple as he'd noticed her toenails were painted last night.

"That's my office." She pointed to a closed door on her left. "I don't use it too often. I prefer to get everything done while I'm at the foundation. Feel free to use it while you're here." She walked a little further before opening a door. Switching on the overhead light, she wheeled his suitcase inside.

"You'll be living here for a while, so if you want to redecorate I don't mind."

His gaze fell on the king-size bed, and ideas of all the ways they could have fun in it assaulted him. And although his brain knew it would never happen tonight, his body had other notions. Before the night was through, he'd be enjoying an ice-cold shower.

"I'm going to change while you unpack. Then we can decide on dinner."

He watched her exit the room before turning his attention to his new home. Various shades of red dominated the room, including the bedding. If he'd been decorating the bedroom, he would have gone with a different color. He saw no reason to change it though, since with any luck his stay in here would only be temporary while he lived with Courtney.

"Brilliant, just brilliant," Courtney muttered as she tossed clothes in a bag intended for the dry cleaners. It would be hard enough to sleep every night knowing Josh was under the same roof, but knowing he was just a few steps away would make it impossible. When he told her to put him anywhere, she should have stuck him in the guest room on the opposite side of the penthouse, as far away from her as possible.

"At least I put him in a guest room," she told the reflection in the mirror.

The bad girl in her, the side she'd only ever let out once and that had been in Hawaii, had urged her to escort him to her bedroom so she could enjoy all the perks of their current arrangement. And she'd been half a breath away from doing it. The only reason she hadn't was because she wasn't sure if mixing sex into their bizarre situation would be a good idea. Until Courtney decided, she planned to keep the bad girl in her gagged. Well, she at least planned to try. Since her hormones went into overdrive every time they were in the same room together, it might be a battle she'd eventually lose. Tonight she would not worry about what might happen in another few days. She would focus on getting through dinner.

She hated living out of a suitcase. Whenever she traveled, regardless of how long she planned to stay, she unpacked. Since this was now his home, she'd expected him to unpack before he did anything else, but either he held the world record for emptying suitcases or he'd left it for later, because he stood in the living room, his cell phone against his ear when she entered. While he might not have unpacked, he'd changed out of the sweater he'd been wearing and into a dark green T-shirt that showcased his broad shoulders and sculpted arms. Jeans, which he'd never worn when they were together in December, hugged his lean hips and long legs, and her palms itched to slip into his back pockets.

"Dad, I understand. But I'm not changing my mind," Josh said, turning his head in her direction.

She'd missed the first part of their conversation, but she had a good idea of what they were talking about.

"Have fun on vacation, and we'll talk when you and Laura get back." Ending the call, he slipped the device into his back pocket.

Lucky phone. Clearing her throat, she forced the thought away. "Is everything okay?"

He rubbed a hand across his sexy barely there beard. Oh, how she'd love to feel it against her thighs again as he—

Stop. Right. There. The last thing she needed was to let her mind wander down that particular avenue while he was standing only a few feet away.

"Dad wanted to share his opinion about our wedding date again."

"Let me guess, he thinks it's too soon." She didn't know how their parents would get along, but at least they had one thing in common. "I got a similar response from my mother." Courtney gestured toward the kitchen. If they sat in there, she could put an entire island between them. "I'm surprised my dad hasn't called to tell me the same thing yet." Since he hadn't, Courtney assumed her mom hadn't shared the news with him.

Opening a drawer, she pulled out all the takeout menus she had. While she was a decent cook and often prepared her own meals, tonight seemed like a good night to have someone else do all the work.

"Pick a place." She handed him the menus before hopping on the stool across from him.

Rather than look through them, he slid them back across to her. "You decide."

What was he up to? She'd spent enough time with him to know he wasn't this easygoing, yet since she walked into his brother's office yesterday, he'd left every decision up to her.

"Are you trying to earn brownie points or something? So

far you've left everything up to me, including the wedding date."

"Depends. Is it working?" he asked with a wink.

"I can't answer that until I know what you plan to use the points for." She selected the menu for her favorite pizza place in the city, well at least her favorite one that would deliver, as well as the one for the best Indian restaurant in Providence. "Which do you prefer?" She held them both up for him to see. "If you don't answer me, I'll take away any brownie points you might have earned."

His fingers brushed against her hands as he took both menus, and a shiver traveled up both arms and down her spine. Like a jack in the box, she bolted off the stool. "While you look them over, I'll get us something to drink." *And maybe I'll look you over*, she mentally added. She didn't bother to ask what he wanted. More than likely he'd give her an answer similar to all his other ones tonight.

"If you really don't care, pizza sounds good."

She traded him the menu for a bottle of sparkling water. "You've earned yourself one point since I felt more like pizza tonight."

The grin he gave her almost stopped her heart, and she resisted the urge to use the menu as a fan. "I've got to start somewhere, and one point is better than none," he said.

Like an idiot, she nodded. "I left my phone in the other room." A moment or two alone might help get her hormones back in order, otherwise she risked hopping onto his lap.

Before she managed to escape, he stood and pulled his cell from his pocket. "Use mine." He held out the device, leaving her no choice but to accept it and make the call from the kitchen, forcing her hormones to remain in chaos.

She kept her eyes focused on the menu as she placed their order, but she didn't need to be looking at him to know he had his eyes locked on her. Every cell in her body knew his gaze lingered on her. In return, the gentle butterflies that had been flying around since she got home tonight turned into soaring eagles.

"They'll be here in about thirty minutes." Handing the phone back to him, she made the mistake of meeting his gaze. There was no missing the spark of interest in his green eyes. It was the same look she'd seen there the afternoon he'd joined her by the rooftop pool. The only difference being that tonight his T-shirt made his eyes an even more brilliant shade of green.

"My parents are expecting us on Saturday. Mom was disappointed I hadn't introduced you to the family yet. Since my brother and his family will be in town this weekend, it seemed like as good a time as any. I already let Addie know we won't be able to make it."

It wasn't the only thing her mom had been disappointed about, but there was no point in sharing all of her mom's views, especially the one regarding whether or not Josh was the type of person she should be marrying. "Since Uncle Mark is doing the ceremony, we can hold the wedding and reception anywhere we want."

You're in big trouble if you say it's up to me. Curious to see what he'd do, she kept the thought to herself.

"I'm open to ideas," he said, "but if it's available, Cliff House would be at the top of my list."

"You earned yourself another point. Cliff House was on my list. I'll call my cousin Callie tomorrow and see if we can use it." Since Uncle Warren had much more important responsibilities, his oldest daughter handled everything pertaining to the mansion. Traditionally the mansion always passed down to the current owner's eldest son. However, her cousin Jake had already made it known he didn't want it, so eventually, the mansion would belong to Callie. "I don't think it'll be a problem."

Courtney crossed one more item off her mental to-do list. "What are your plans for tomorrow?"

"Don't have any at the moment."

"We need to get a marriage license. I have some free time in the afternoon. If you have your birth certificate, we can go to City Hall before lunch and get it." Most people didn't carry their birth certificate around, but since he'd planned this whole arrangement out before yesterday, he might have come to Rhode Island prepared.

Josh's cell phone buzzed. Shaking his head, he glanced at the screen but didn't pick up the device. "It's in Maine. Instead of waiting until the weekend, I'll drive up tomorrow and get it and everything else I need."

As much as she wanted to visit Bar Harbor, maybe letting him make the trip alone was a better idea. If she went with him, it would mean being trapped in the same car with him for a minimum of ten hours round trip, and who knew what kind of effect that would have on her decision to keep the bad girl in her gagged.

AFTER READJUSTING HER PILLOW, Courtney flipped on her back and stared into the darkness. She wasn't sure exactly how long she'd been in bed, but it felt like hours. Hours of staring into the darkness while her mind remained centered on the bedroom down the hall. Okay, well not the bedroom but the man sleeping in there. The one she'd teased and joked with while they watched a movie after dinner. The one who sat next to her and somehow managed to touch her countless times. Sometimes it had been his leg brushing against hers when he shifted his position. Other times it had been his arm as he scratched an itch. No matter where the contact happened, it left her skin tingling. She'd finally gone to bed, not because she was tired, but to get away from Josh before she gave in to the temptation and kissed him.

Unfortunately, the distance wasn't helping. Instead of falling asleep or concentrating on what awaited her at the office tomorrow, Courtney kept thinking about how much more enjoyable Josh could make her time in bed. Thanks to all her firsthand knowledge, she knew the precise answer.

"I give up." Courtney switched on the bedside lamp and kicked off the blankets. She'd make a cup of tea and watch television. While neither one always put her to sleep when insomnia struck, they helped pass the time. Tonight maybe she would get really lucky and the combination would distract her enough to get in a few hours of sleep.

With a cup of freshly brewed chamomile tea in hand, Courtney scrolled through the classic episodes of *I Love Lucy*. While the show might be outdated in many ways, it still made her laugh. Often when she had a lot on her mind and couldn't sleep, she switched on an episode, even though at this point she'd seen them all numerous times. After selecting the episode where Lucy and Ethel got jobs at a candy factory, she tugged a throw blanket over her legs and willed thoughts of Josh from her mind.

"That's one of my favorite episodes."

It would be nice if the voice was all in her head, but she knew it wasn't. *So much for using the television as a distraction.*

Courtney looked away from the screen, where Fred was showing Ricky the cake he'd made while the women were at work, and toward the door. If she'd had trouble falling asleep before, seeing Josh in the doorway in just a pair of shorts ruled out any chance it'd happen at all tonight. Her memories didn't do Josh justice. Part of her brain urged her to keep focused on his face. The other gave her the green light to look wherever she wanted. After all, he was the one who'd decided to walk around half-naked, not her. Courtney's eyes knew which argument they preferred. Slowly they traveled past his chest, down his abdomen, and lower. Although it was perhaps the worst idea ever, they lingered on the taut ridge his shorts simply couldn't hide, and heat that had nothing to do with embarrassment rushed to every part of her body.

"Can I join you?" Josh asked rather than make himself at home.

"Sure." *Just sit anywhere but next to me.* "You've watched *I Love Lucy?*"

Clearly, Josh had his mind reading abilities turned off tonight, because rather than sit in one of the multiple other places in the room, he dropped down on the sofa next to her. Even though they weren't touching, the heat from his body managed to seep into hers, pushing her internal temperature even higher.

Josh stretched his legs out and crossed his ankles. "I don't think I've seen all the episodes, but I've watched a lot of them. My favorite is the one where Lucy makes the commercial for the vitameatavegamin."

Who didn't love that episode? It was a classic.

She should finish this episode and retreat to the safety of her bedroom. She already knew that wasn't what she would do. "I'll put it on next."

BESIDE HIM, Courtney leaned forward for her cup of what looked like tea, and the neck of her oversized T-shirt slipped off one shoulder, exposing the tiny birthmark at the very top of her right breast. The one that usually remained hidden under her clothes. If her shirt somehow dipped another few inches, her nipple would be free.

The image of him reaching over and pulling the shirt down played out in his mind. Once he had the fabric out of the way, he'd lower his mouth to her dusky pink nipple while his other hand slipped beneath the blanket covering her lap and settled between her legs.

Not tonight. Rather than move the top down and carry out the fantasy playing out in his head, Josh grabbed the shirt's neckline and tugged it back into place. Then he readjusted his position on the sofa, putting several more inches between them.

"Can't sleep?" he asked. For all he knew, drinking tea and watching old sitcom reruns might be part of her normal routine at home. If it was, he'd have to think twice the next time insomnia struck, and he went wandering around.

Courtney sipped her tea as she shook her head. "I keep thinking about how the media will react tomorrow." Instead of putting the cup back where it had been, she held on to it in her lap. "You?"

Yeah, no way was he telling her the cause of his inability to sleep. Despite the frigid shower he took before bed, the damn erection refused to quit. It probably didn't help that his body knew the cure for the problem was sleeping under the same roof. "Same."

"Since when do you care about the media?"

Talk about being caught in a lie. "I don't care what they say about me. I'm worried about how this might affect you."

While it wasn't what was keeping him up, it wasn't a lie either. Some people did everything they could to get the kind of attention Courtney was about to get, and they knew just how to handle it. Courtney might say she was prepared, but no one truly knew how they would react until put in the position. While his ex-girlfriend Naomi, who had once worked for his dad, loved the perks of being with him, she'd hated the regular scrutiny of their relationship. The stories that had regularly popped up in the tabloids while they were together claiming he was cheating on her hadn't helped their relationship either, even though they'd all been false. He had one-night stands and short weekend flings, but never while they were together. He wasn't a cheater. There were some lines even he wouldn't cross.

She looked away from the television and at him. "If I were you, I'd be more worried about meeting my dad and brother Saturday."

Her expression gave him no clue as to whether she was being serious or joking around. Either way, he'd find out in a few days.

SEVEN

Bacon? Why did Josh smell bacon? His brother hated the stuff. Even if Evan did cook breakfast for himself, which he never did, his brother wouldn't be cooking bacon. Opening his eyes, Josh glanced around, momentarily confused by what he saw. He smelled bacon because he wasn't at his brother's condo. He was at Courtney's place. More specifically, he was on the sofa in nothing but shorts.

Josh tossed the blanket covering him aside. He had no idea how it had ended up on top of him. The last thing he remembered, they'd been watching his favorite *I Love Lucy* episode, and Courtney was using the blanket. Now she was gone, the television was turned off, and he had a cramp in his neck that told him he'd been sleeping there for some time.

He rolled his head, hoping to loosen up his neck, and stood. If he smelled bacon, she had either made breakfast or was in the process of making it. Either way, it meant she was no longer in bed.

Except for the open laptop, a plate of food, and the full French press, the kitchen was empty. Josh doubted she'd left for the day though. While he sometimes left a plate behind for someone else to deal with, everything he knew about her told him she would not. While he waited for her to return, he'd help himself to some coffee.

On Monday night she'd served him some. Which cupboard had she taken the cup from? He reached for the one closest to the refrigerator.

"Hey, you're up. I hope I didn't wake you."

At the sound of her voice, he turned. The only difference between the way she looked now and when he'd stumbled upon her last night was her hair. Rather than leave it loose, she'd tied it up in a messy bun. His first instinct was to walk over, pull out the hair elastic, and run his fingers through it.

"The coffee cups are in the next cupboard." She retook her seat at the kitchen island and put down the cell phone and coffee cup in her hand. "If I'd known you'd be up soon, I would have made enough breakfast for both of us."

Eggs were okay. He'd eat them, but they weren't his favorite. Some of the bacon on her plate would have been nice. "I'm happy with cereal if you have any."

"Sorry. I'm not a big cereal fan. But if you want to make a list of foods you like, I'll add them to my order. It'll be delivered on Friday."

How could anyone not like cereal? He'd have to make sure some found its way into the kitchen today. For now, there was a loaf of bread on the counter. "Do you have any peanut butter?" A person couldn't go wrong with some peanut butter toast.

"It's in the third cupboard to your right on the top shelf." She picked up her fork, but before she could use it, her cell phone chimed. After typing a reply, she set it back down. "I tried to wake you before I went to bed, but you were dead to the world. Did you ever make it back to your room?"

"No." The cramp in his neck would remind him of where he'd slept all day too.

Her cell phone chimed again. This time she ignored it and stabbed a slice of bacon. "Are you still going to drive up to Maine and get your things?"

Right, he had said he would go and get his birth certificate today. "If I go today, we can apply for the marriage license tomorrow."

"Before I leave, I'll give you a key so you can get in." She silenced the cell phone when it rang. "I'm supposed to go to Meg's for book club tonight, so if I'm not here when you get home, that's where I am." She scooped up a forkful of scrambled eggs. "But I'm thinking about skipping it."

Peanut butter toast in hand, he took the stool opposite her. "Don't skip because of me. I don't mind being here alone."

"You're not the reason—well, you are sort of the reason I might not go. I'm not sure I'm up for a grilling from Meg, Celeste, and Rebecca. And I know I'll get one." She turned the laptop, so the screen faced him. A picture of them together in Hawaii dominated the website, along with a headline announcing their engagement. In addition to the picture of them together, there were two smaller headshots of each of them.

"It's not even seven yet and already I have gotten messages and calls from my friends."

The article on the *Today Magazine* website had gone live only an hour ago according to the date and time stamp below the headline, so technically Pauline had waited until today to send out the press release.

Pulling the laptop closer, Josh scanned the article, which told the exact story they'd come up with. The only thing not mentioned in the article was the date and location of the wedding, since he hadn't known it when he spoke with Pauline.

"Feel free to check any other site you want," she said.

Maybe he would later. For now, he'd rather have a conversation with the woman sitting across from him. The one who was giving up a lot to help him. "Unless I hit a lot of traffic, I should be back here by seven. If you decide not to go to Meg's, let me know and I'll pick up takeout on the way home. We can hang out and watch some more *I Love Lucy* or whatever you want."

"You're desperate for more brownie points, aren't you?" Amusement flickered in her eyes. "When I decide, I'll let you know."

Courtney finished her breakfast and took a final sip of coffee. As he expected, she added the plate and cup to the dishwasher. "Have a nice day."

She touched his bare shoulder as she spoke, and before his brain could tell his arm no, it went around her waist. Fully intent on kissing her, Josh pulled her in closer. His brain got the message to the rest of him just in time though, and instead of kissing her slightly parted lips, he kissed her cheek.

"You too. See you tonight."

Josh watched her walk away. What would she do it if he followed her and offered to help her in the shower? They'd shared more than one shower in Hawaii.

Bad idea. Josh dropped his gaze back to his peanut butter toast. If he made such an offer, she might tell him the deal was off and insist he pack up his bags. He couldn't risk it. If—no, not if but when—he'd seen the way she looked at him and didn't doubt their relationship would turn intimate again—it happened, she would be the one to make the first move.

COURTNEY RUBBED her eyes and then turned her chair so she could look out her office window. Much like on the drive into work earlier, the sky remained gray and overcast. According to the forecast, they were only supposed to receive rain today.

While it might be correct, it certainly looked and felt like the powdery stuff was on its way. Although the area had received snow early this winter, it'd been more than two weeks since they'd received a single snowflake. If it were up to her, it would stay that way. As far as the fluffy white stuff went, the only time she wanted it was when she was skiing—an activity she participated in only a handful of times each year because she'd much rather vacation on a sandy beach than a snow-covered mountain. Josh, she knew, loved both locations, which helped explain why he considered Maine his primary residence despite the fact he had no family living in the area.

It's not his primary residence anymore, she reminded herself. Last night when he'd fallen asleep, she'd tried several times to wake him. Each time, he'd mumbled something incoherent and kept on sleeping. Eventually, she gave up and covered him with a blanket. Then she'd climbed back into bed and hoped the next time she saw him, he had on more clothes. Naturally, that hadn't happened. Instead, she'd walked back into the kitchen and found him standing there in just his shorts as if he'd been doing it forever. Much like when she saw him last night, she'd given her eyes the okay to enjoy the view. She'd also been half a breath away from allowing her hands to skim over his chest and down his torso. Judging by the way he watched her, Josh wouldn't have stopped her either. If he went around the penthouse like that every night and each morning, she wasn't sure how long she'd be able to restrain the bad girl lurking inside her.

The knock on the door caused the memory of Josh this morning to disappear. Turning her chair away from the window, she said, "Come in."

Both her younger sister and Terry, one of the office assistants, stepped inside.

"Ms. Belmont, I've Marcy Blake on the phone. She'd like to speak with you," Terry said.

Even if her sister wasn't standing there, she'd rather not take a call from the reporter from *Today Magazine*. While she couldn't avoid Marcy forever, she could at least put her off for now. "Please let her know I'm unavailable at the moment and tell her she can try back tomorrow."

"I will. And, Ms. Belmont, congratulations on the engagement," Terry said before closing the door.

She'd been receiving similar comments from everyone at the foundation today.

Juliette didn't bother with a polite hello or a "how are you?" Instead, she sat in the chair on the other side of the desk and got right to the point. "I've been calling you all day."

She'd turned the ringer on her cell phone off around lunchtime and stuck the device in her desk drawer. While she understood her family and friends' curiosity, the constant calls and text messages made getting anything done impossible.

"It would have been nice if you'd told me you were engaged. Instead, I had to read about it like everyone else."

"I called you."

After her meeting with her mom, she'd called both her brother and sister. When Juliette didn't answer, she'd left a message. It wasn't Courtney's fault her sister never called back.

"I got home late yesterday." Juliette moved to the edge of the chair and crossed her arms on the desk. "So you've been with Josh since the summer? When those pictures showed up in December, I should have known there was something going on between the two of you. A two-week fling with him never quite seemed right. It was too much like something I'd do."

If her sister, who knew her better than anyone, was buying the story they'd concocted, everyone else, including Josh's ex, should be too.

"Why didn't you tell me? You know it would have stayed between us," Juliette asked.

She heard and understood the reason for the disappointment in her sister's voice. While they were as different as two sisters could possibly be, they were close. Before this, Courtney couldn't recall ever keeping anything important from Juliette.

"I made Josh promise not to tell anyone until I was ready. It didn't seem right for me to tell even you if he couldn't tell his family."

"Still, I can't believe you've been with him since July and you managed to keep it a secret. How did you do it?"

Unlike Courtney, Juliette was no stranger to the media. While Courtney and Scott resembled their dad, Juliette inherited her looks from their mom, and there was no mistaking that she was a member of the Sherbrooke family. Actually, she and their cousin Sara looked more like sisters than cousins. Thanks to Juliette's appearance and the fact she liked to have fun, she often appeared on the cover of various tabloids and her modeling kept her picture just about everywhere else.

Good question. One she should've anticipated and already come up with a plausible answer to.

"We spent most of our time at either my apartment in Boston or whatever hotel he was staying in. When we went to someplace public, we never arrived or left together. We did the same thing coming and going from my apartment and his hotels. Plus, I think we just got a bit lucky."

"A bit? Talk about an understatement."

Juliette reached for Courtney's left hand and examined the ring masquerading as her engagement ring. Even if her sister had seen it on her before, she didn't think Juliette would remember it. Still, Courtney held her breath.

"Well, he knows what you like." Juliette placed her hands on the desk. "Have you set a date?"

"February first. I'm going to ask Callie if we can use Cliff House." She'd left a message for Callie earlier today. "And before you say anything, I mean next month, not February of next year."

"After all these years, I'm finally rubbing off on you," Juliette said with a smile. If a rushed wedding was anyone's style, it was Juliette's. "Did you tell Mom yet?"

Courtney nodded. "She wasn't pleased, especially since she hasn't met Josh. Saturday night we're going to Mom and Dad's for dinner. Scott and Paige will be there too. Mom said she would call and invite you so everyone can meet him before the wedding."

"She left me a voice mail earlier. I haven't had a chance to call her back. But I met Josh last year at one of Seth Vallencourt's parties. If Selena Cruise hadn't been draped all over him, I would have tried to get to know him better."

Courtney knew exactly what Juliette meant by "get to know him better." Her sister was the female version of a playboy and went through more boyfriends in a year than she'd had in her lifetime.

A sharp jab of jealousy struck her in the chest at the thought of either Selena or her sister with Josh.

"We didn't talk for a long time, but he seemed like a nice guy." Juliette continued while Courtney struggled with the image of Selena Cruise, an actress well-known for her mile-long legs and size D breasts, hanging all over Josh.

"I'll call Mom later and let her know I'll be there on Saturday."

You don't have to come, she thought as Juliette replaced Selena in the image tormenting her. She didn't consider herself the jealous type. This afternoon, the ugly emotion was messing with her head.

"Next month. That doesn't give us a lot of time to find you a dress."

If she was about to marry someone she expected to spend the rest of her life with, she'd want every aspect of the day to be perfect, including her gown. This marriage had an undetermined expiration date, and while she wanted to look nice, she wasn't concerned about finding *the* dress. For the sake of their charade, she'd play along.

"Unless you already have someone working on it, I don't think there is enough time to have something custom designed. You'll have to buy something off the rack."

"You make it sound like the worst thing in the world."

Her sister shrugged. "I guess it's not, but do you really want a gown hundreds of other women have worn? I'd rather have something unique."

"Off the rack will be fine."

"If you say so," Juliette said, tapping her fingers against the desktop. "Can you take tomorrow off? We can head into New York or Boston and shop."

"There are bridal stores in Rhode Island." She enjoyed a good shopping trip in New York as much as the next person, but she'd prefer not to make the drive anytime soon.

Juliette rolled her eyes. "Please. We won't find anything around here. So what do you say?"

She didn't have any meetings scheduled for tomorrow, and she did need a wedding dress. "Sure, but let's go into Boston."

WHEN THE SNOWFLAKES started coming down while he packed his bags, Josh considered spending the night in Bar Harbor rather than drive back to Providence. The text he received from Courtney while digging out his birth certificate letting him know she wasn't going to her friend's made the final decision for him.

Once out of Maine, the snow changed to a messy wintery mix and stayed that way for much of the ride. By the time he reached Providence though, it turned back to all snow, but at least so far there was little accumulation on the ground. If the steady stream continued all night however, it would be a very different story in the morning.

As promised, he stopped for takeout on the way back to the Mayfair—a task he should've known would take far longer than necessary today of all days. Although his publicist had been selective of which media sites she told about their engagement, the news had quickly spread to others, including perhaps his least favorite of them all, the *Star Insider*.

When he walked in the penthouse, the lights were on in both the kitchen and the living room, but Courtney wasn't in either. This morning he'd left before Courtney, but he didn't think she would leave them on all day. So if the lights were on, she was here.

"Courtney," he called, setting down the bags of food and removing the items inside. When silence answered him, he passed through the living room and down the hall. Both her bedroom and office doors were closed. He knocked on the bedroom door first. Again he got no response. Moving down the hall, he rapped his knuckles on the office door.

"Hey. Have you been home long?" Courtney asked from her bedroom doorway.

Her wet hair hung loose, and she was wearing flannel pajama bottoms and a cropped white V-neck T-shirt that didn't quite reach her waist. Unlike last night's shirt that was oversized, this one fit snugly, and thanks to the wet spots created by her hair, he could see the outline of her nips through the fabric.

Josh forced his eyes away from the tantalizing view and met her eyes. "Uh, no. I just got here. You?" Needing to do something with his hands before they got him in trouble, he shoved them in his pockets.

Courtney closed the door and walked in his direction.

"Got home about an hour and a half ago. I hoped some time in the Jacuzzi would help me relax. It was a crazy day."

He wouldn't mind a soak in the Jacuzzi either, with or without her. After so much time in the car driving, his back and shoulders were tight. Unfortunately, his bathroom didn't contain one. "Did it?" He followed her into the kitchen, careful to keep his eyes trained on the back of her head.

"A little." Opening a cupboard, she reached up for the plates, causing her shirt to ride up. Like a moth drawn to light, his eyes locked on the bare skin now on display. "What did you get us?" She put the plates down near the takeout containers before getting out silverware.

With her back again turned toward him, he tried to adjust himself. Had she picked the pajama top to intentionally torture him? If so, it was working. "Thai from Sweet Ginger. I hope that's okay."

"I haven't had a chance to try there yet." She added a little from each container to her plate. "Let's eat in the other room and watch television."

Josh took his time filling his plate and grabbed two bottles of sparkling water from the refrigerator. When he joined her in what most would consider a family room, Courtney already had the television on and she was scrolling through old *I Love Lucy* episodes.

"Any requests?" she asked him.

Oh, he had a request all right, but it had nothing to do with what they watched while eating dinner. "Surprise me." He considered one of the overstuffed chairs. It would be the safest place in the room to sit. Josh walked past the one closest to him and joined Courtney on the sofa.

The only sound in the room came from the flat-screen television mounted on the wall while they ate. Or more specifically in Josh's case, while he ate and envisioned removing Courtney's top so he could see more than just the outline of her nipples. If any erotic images were going through her head, she didn't let on.

"Callie said we can use Cliff House for the wedding. She offered to help with any planning too, and I already called Henri. He'll call me back soon with some menu ideas. Did you get everything you needed today?" She opened the bottle of water he'd brought in for her.

"Yeah. We can go to City Hall tomorrow for the marriage license."

"We'll have to go on Friday. I'm going shopping for a wedding dress in Boston with my sister tomorrow."

"I'm surprised you're not going to New York."

"She wanted to, but I don't feel like it. There are plenty of bridal stores in Boston. I won't have a problem finding something."

For about the fifth time since sitting down, he rubbed his neck and rolled it from side to side.

"Stiff neck?"

It wasn't the only thing that was stiff tonight. Josh nodded. "My neck and back were already bothering me this morning. All the time in the car didn't help."

Setting aside her water, she moved onto her knees. "Take off your shirt and turn around. I'll give you a back rub. It might help."

If she put her hands on him, he could kiss any chance of sleeping tonight goodbye, so the smart thing to do would be to politely decline. Unlike Courtney, who'd graduated both high school and college early, he wasn't smart. Grabbing the bottom of his shirt, Josh pulled it over his head.

Energy sizzled and cracked across his skin when her palms came down on his shoulders. Slowly, she kneaded and massaged the tight muscles in his upper back. He'd had plenty of massages in his life, especially when he was prepping for a role and spent countless hours in the gym. None had ever affected him the way this one was. While Courtney was working out the knots almost as well as any professional, her touch was acting like gasoline to a fire. With each movement of her hands, his body tightened and his internal temperature inched higher.

She kneaded a particularly tight spot, and he moaned.

"I'll assume you're enjoying the massage," she said as audience laughter erupted from the television.

Closing his eyes, he allowed himself to enjoy the feel of her skin against his for the first time after so many weeks.

She shifted her position, her body rubbing against his, and he felt her pebbled nipples against his back as she trailed her fingers up and over his shoulders. Her touch was more of a caress than a massage now. Gradually her hands slipped lower, and he held his breath as they passed his clavicle and stopped.

Moist lips touched the back of his neck. Before he could react, Courtney's hands moved lower, and he dug down deep for the control necessary not to turn and take over. A second kiss joined the first, and her palms caressed his skin as they moved back toward his shoulders. Then just like that, they disappeared, as did the weight of her body leaning against him. Prepared to ask what was wrong, Josh turned, expecting to find Courtney back in a sitting position. Instead, he found her still kneeling and pulling her top off.

Erect nipples taunted him, begging him to touch them. Despite his efforts, his self-control started to slip. He placed his hands on her sides mere inches below her breasts, because if he touched them he was a goner. "Courtney." His voice came out strangled.

She met and held his gaze while her fingers undid the button on his jeans and tugged the zipper down. Her hand closed around him as he took possession of her mouth.

"Any better?" Her voice broke through the vivid daydream playing out in his head.

"Much." Although it'd been all in his head, he could almost feel her hand wrapped around him.

"Do you want me to keep going?"

If she kept going, the little self-control he had left would be long gone. "No. I'm good. Thanks."

Her hands disappeared from his body, and she sat down again. After pulling his shirt back on, Josh reached for his plate, glad Courtney's attention was on the television and not him, because if she took one look at him, she'd know exactly what was on his mind.

EIGHT

WHEN COURTNEY OFFERED TO GIVE JOSH A BACK RUB Wednesday night, she'd done so because she wanted to help, not because she wanted to touch him. Well, it had been mostly because she wanted to help. Either way, it hadn't taken long for her to realize what a gigantic mistake it was. Once she touched his skin, memories of his hands moving across her body forced their way front and center, as did memories of her pleasuring him. Abruptly stopping the massage would have seemed strange, so she'd gritted her teeth and suffered through it. Alone in bed later, she'd wondered what the hell was wrong with her. They were both adults and physically attracted to each other. Denying herself the pleasure she knew full well Josh could give her because there was a miniscule chance she might let her guard down and get emotionally attached was plain stupid. She was an intelligent woman. If she didn't want to let her emotions into play, she wouldn't.

Simple.

She'd had the same argument with herself on Thursday and then again last night after climbing into bed very much alone while Josh retreated to his bedroom down the hall.

Much to his credit, Josh had been a perfect gentleman since he moved in. Although he still appeared in the kitchen without a shirt in the morning, he always kept his hands and his lips to himself, despite the clear evidence he wanted more than a companion to eat meals with while they watched reruns of old black-and-white sitcoms.

Would she be having the same talk with herself tonight? As much as she'd like to say no, she knew more than likely she'd be alone in the big bed again when they came back from her parents'. While she'd somehow managed it in Hawaii by inviting Josh back to her room, she wasn't comfortable making the first move. But if she wanted them to return to the intimate relationship they'd had, she'd need to do just that, since Josh seemed intent on leaving the status of their relationship in her corner.

The knock on her door put her current thoughts on hold.

Although they'd shared breakfast every morning since he moved in, she was the first one in the kitchen. Josh always joined her before she finished pouring her first cup of coffee. She didn't know if he set his alarm so he was up before she left or if he was simply a morning person who liked to get up early. Whichever it was, she enjoyed having the company.

"Courtney." Josh's voice traveled through the closed door.

Thus far this week, their bedrooms had remained off-limits, so if he was outside the door now, there must be a good reason. "I'm up. Come on in." She set aside the book she'd been reading—well, trying to read. She was still on the same page as when she'd picked it up twenty minutes ago.

She held her breath as the door opened. Considering where her thoughts were before he interrupted, she didn't know if she could handle a shirtless Josh in her bedroom this morning.

A fully dressed Josh appeared in the doorway, but he didn't step into the room. "I made breakfast for us."

Unless you counted picking up takeout, in the past four days, he'd exhibited no culinary skills whatsoever. Something along the lines of "you cooked?" almost slipped out, but she stopped herself just in time. No matter what was waiting for her in the kitchen, it was the thought that counted.

"Great. I'm hungry." She tossed aside the throw blanket she'd been using since she sat down in the chair and gave the bed a wide berth as she headed for the door.

He'd put a plate containing what looked like an egg and cheese omelet near the seat she usually used at the island. A bowl full of some kind of sugary cereal was in Josh's preferred spot. Fresh fruit, an assortment of baked goods, and coffee completed the meal.

"How long have you been up?" she asked as she sat. Yesterday her grocery order had contained a large assortment of fruit but not a single muffin or cinnamon roll. So either he'd gone out for the ingredients to make them, which she doubted, or he'd made a trip to a local bakery.

"A few hours. I thought you might like breakfast when you got up." He poured milk into the bowl of cereal. She wasn't sure what kind he was eating today, but based on the color, it was chocolate flavored. She wasn't sure if that was better or worse than the marshmallow-laced one he'd eaten yesterday with a side of bacon. "I made the omelet, but the muffins and cinnamon rolls are from Ambrosia."

She eyed her plate. "Thanks. It looks delicious." Courtney hoped it tasted as good as it looked, but if it didn't, she'd never tell him. With her fork, she cut off a corner and tentatively popped it in her mouth. In her opinion, it needed a little more salt, but otherwise the omelet tasted great. "You didn't make yourself an omelet?"

Josh covered his cereal with slices of banana, as if adding fruit to the bowl would somehow make it any healthier. "Not a big fan of eggs." He scooped up a spoonful of cereal and popped it in his mouth, then reached for one of the oversized cinnamon rolls.

They'd eaten breakfast together almost every morning in Hawaii. Now that she thought about it, he'd always ordered carb-heavy meals like pancakes and waffles. Various types of breakfast meats had usually accompanied his meals.

"Do you want to split this with me?" He pointed to the bakery treat with his knife.

She knew from past experiences just how tasty the roll was. It was also huge, and she'd never be able to eat an entire one and her omelet. "Sure."

No sooner did the bakery treat appear on her plate than Courtney cut into it. A rich combination of cinnamon, brown sugar, and icing melted on her tongue. After cutting off another piece, she eyed it and then her omelet. The one Josh had taken the time to make, but she'd barely touched. Rather than enjoy another bite of the cinnamon roll, she returned to the eggs.

"What time do we need to be at your parents'?" Josh asked between mouthfuls of food.

The question barely registered, thanks to the dab of icing on his lips. All she needed to do was lean to the right and she'd be able to lick it off. Who knew where things would go from there?

"Uh, around five." She started to lean in his direction.

He raised another spoonful of cereal toward his mouth, and she wasn't sure if she should thank or curse the silly utensil that now stood between her and his lips.

"Do you have any plans until then?" he asked.

"Unless hanging around here and being lazy counts, nope." Grabbing a napkin, Courtney held it out. "You have icing on your lip."

Rather than wipe his mouth, Josh licked the icing off. If she suddenly had some of the same sugary goodness on her lip or perhaps another part of her body, would Josh be kind enough to lick it off for her?

"The ice rink opens soon. How do you feel about ice skating this afternoon?"

Located not far from City Hall in Kennedy Plaza, the outdoor rink was used year-round. In the winter people could ice skate or participate in ice bumper cars. During the warmer months, people used the area for a wide range of activities as well. She'd passed by the rink countless times, but she'd never had any desire to visit.

"I don't own any skates." She couldn't remember the last time she slipped on ice skates.

"I checked the website when I got back because I don't have any here either, and we can rent some there." Josh selected what appeared to be a blueberry muffin from the assortment and added it to his plate. "We don't have to go. I just thought it might be fun."

She'd never been a great skater, but when she'd been younger she usually managed to stay on her feet even if it hadn't always been pretty. It'd been a long time since she tried though. If she attempted it today, there was a high probability she'd spend most of her time on her butt. Still, it might help cement their charade in the eyes of the public. Not once since they announced their engagement had they been spotted together. If a couple really was in love and about to be married, shouldn't they be seen together as often as possible?

"It's been a very long time since I skated, so before we go, it's only fair to warn you that I'll probably spend a lot of time falling."

In the process of buttering his muffin, Josh paused. "Don't worry. I'll take care of you and make sure you stay on your feet."

REGARDLESS OF THE weather or the temperature, Josh enjoyed spending time outdoors. Unfortunately, he had done little of it over the past several weeks, and the ice rink had been a stark reminder of that fact when he passed by earlier this morning. Any other time, he would head north and enjoy a few days of skiing. With that ruled out as an option this weekend, an hour or two of skating would get him outside. While he could go alone, he'd much rather have Courtney's company, something he looked forward to more and more each day.

If given a choice, Josh didn't get up before eight o'clock, and at the moment he had no place he needed to be each day. Still, he'd set his alarm so he was up in time to enjoy breakfast with Courtney before she left for work. During the day, he found ways to keep himself busy, but she frequently popped into his thoughts. And although the only time he usually sat at home and watched television at night was when he had his daughter with him, he'd looked forward to doing exactly that when Courtney came home since the first night he walked in on her watching old reruns of *I Love Lucy*. Considering the number of episodes they'd watched together over the past few nights, they'd run out before the month was over and need to find something else to do. Josh knew what he'd like that to be. However, until Courtney reached the same conclusion, he'd enjoy spending time with her in whatever way she'd allow, and at the moment that meant skating around the ice rink in the middle of downtown Providence.

While Josh waited for Courtney to finish lacing up her skates, he glanced around the ice rink. Although it had only opened a short while ago, people of all ages were already moving across the ice. So far, except for when the woman working the skate rental desk flat-out asked if he was J.T. Williamson, he'd remained inconspicuous. However, considering the number of people already here, it was only a matter of time before someone snapped a picture or stopped him and asked for an autograph. And if a picture appeared on the internet, Pauline would be doing backflips of joy. She'd sent him several texts over the past few days telling him the media expected pictures of them together. She'd even suggested they stage some photo ops to keep both his fans and the magazines happy. When it came to his personal life, he didn't care what the media expected, so he'd made it clear she wasn't to stage anything. However, he couldn't control what random people with cell phone cameras did when they were out in public.

"Okay, I'm ready." She sounded anything but ready.

Standing, Josh held out his gloved hand. "It'll come back to you. Skating is a lot like riding a bike." He hoped so, anyway. If not, he might be kicking himself later for suggesting the activity today.

"If you say so."

She didn't hesitate to accept his hand as she cautiously came to her feet. She didn't let go as they made their way onto the ice. He didn't know if she kept it there because it helped with her balance or because she wanted the physical contact. Either way, he didn't care. It felt right there.

Josh kept them as close to the wall as possible as they moved at a snail's pace across the ice. Around them, people zoomed past, including kids who looked no older than five or six. If he was alone, he'd feel compelled to not only keep up with the other skaters but to pass them. Not today. Right now he was exactly where he wanted to be, and he didn't care what the people around him were doing.

More than halfway around the ice, Courtney picked up her pace. Rather than moving at the speed of a snail, they were moving about as fast a turtle. They still wouldn't beat any records, but it was an improvement.

"I was hoping the news was wrong, but it looks and feels like it's going to snow," she said as they approached the spot where they'd started.

He'd never be able to explain it to someone who'd never experienced a snowstorm, but he understood exactly what she meant. The air felt like snow was on the way, and he hoped the weather forecast was correct because he loved a good snowstorm. It was one of the many reasons he spent as much of his time as he could in New England.

"At least it's not supposed to start until around midnight. We should be home from my parents' by then." Courtney changed her pace again as they started on their second lap around the rink, and they passed another couple skating.

If the storm started much earlier than expected and forced them to skip dinner, he wouldn't complain. From the little he knew of her family, they were tight. Given what they believed were the facts of their relationship, he didn't expect them to welcome him with open arms tonight—not that he expected them to be hostile. Instead, they'd be aloof but polite. Although he wasn't looking forward to it, he could understand their likely behavior.

"Is your sister going to be there?"

The only time she'd mentioned Juliette was when she announced they were going shopping in Boston for a wedding dress. Before they arrived tonight, he'd like to know who he was about to face across the dinner table.

Courtney glanced at him briefly. "I thought I told you she'd be there."

Josh shook his head. He would have remembered that detail.

"Mom invited my aunts and uncles too. I don't know if they'll make it."

He'd prepared himself for a small gathering. It sounded like her mom had other plans in mind.

"Between you and me, I hope they don't. I love them, but I already know Mom will start in again on pushing the wedding date back. If Aunt Judith is there, I think she'll do the same."

Except for occasionally attending the Christmas party his dad hosted every year, Josh didn't do family gatherings. Perhaps if he liked more of his family, he would, but except for his brother, sister, and dad, he'd never been close to the majority of his relatives. That even included his mom. And he couldn't imagine what it would be like to have a family more like Courtney's.

"You were right about this being like riding a bike. Another few times out here, and I might be able to keep up with those preschoolers over there." Smiling, she nodded toward a group of young children learning to skate. "You don't have to stick by my side while we're here. Going this slow can't be a lot of fun for you."

There's no place I'd rather be. The thought almost knocked him on his ass. But it was true. The only other person he'd want to be spending time with right now was his daughter. "Who says I can skate any faster than this?"

The look she threw him spoke volumes. Before she could add a comment to her expression, a twenty-something-year old woman wearing a New England Rebels snow hat skated in front of them and stopped, forcing them to do the same or crash into her.

Rather than apologize for almost causing a collision, the woman smiled and pulled a cell phone from her jacket pocket. "You really are here. When Fiona texted that she'd rented skates to you, I didn't believe her."

The woman's comment didn't surprise him. But he hoped Fiona hadn't also posted the news on a social media site.

"I've seen all your movies. Can I get a photo of us together?" She didn't wait for an answer before moving into position next to him.

Courtney's fingers slipped from his hand. "I'll take it for you."

Immediately, the fan handed over the device and then put

her arm around his waist. "My sister is going to be so mad when I tell her I met you. She loves you. I thought she was going to cry when she read you were getting married."

Never mind her sister being mad, he was. Thanks to her, other people were taking notice of them. Some we simply staring in their direction, but two people were standing near Courtney with their cell phones in hand. Normally fans didn't bother him. If not for them, he wouldn't have a career. This afternoon, he wished he didn't have a single fan in the world.

"I took a couple for you." Courtney handed the phone back to the woman, who remained glued to his side.

"Thanks." Although she removed her arm, she didn't leave. "Could I take a picture of you for my sister?"

Josh shot Courtney a look intended to tell her he was sorry before answering.

A similar scenario played out with the other two fans. As soon as they left, he grabbed Courtney's hand and started moving again. The women he dated knew there was a possibility that fans or photographers would seek him out. When it happened, he never felt the need to apologize to them. Today he did.

"I'm sorry."

HE HAD nothing to be sorry for. Since the moment they'd met, Courtney had known he was one of the biggest male actors around. She'd seen fans approach him countless times while in Hawaii and ask for a few pictures and often an autograph. People wouldn't suddenly lose interest in him because they were no longer in paradise.

Some conversations you needed to have face-to-face. Courtney skated in front of him and stopped. "Sorry? Why, because those fans came over to you? I knew it would happen eventually." Moving closer, she placed her palms on his shoulders. "You don't need to apologize."

She intended to kiss him on the cheek. Give him a friendly, sisterly kiss to let him know she wasn't upset. Somehow the message got changed before it reached its final destination, and her lips brushed against his instead.

Considering the outside temperature, his lips should be cold. Instead, they were warm and, in a single word, perfect.

The gag slipped off the bad girl in her, and she spoke up. *No point in stopping now.*

As if they had a mind of their own, her arms slipped over his shoulders as she moved her mouth against his. With each pass, the rest of the world slipped away a little more. Soon the only things registering were Josh's lips and his body against hers.

A loud wolf whistle brought reality crashing back down around her. She was holding onto Josh as if her life depended on it while having her way with his mouth in a public place filled with people. Clearly, the left side of her brain had turned off for the day. Her sister did things like this. She didn't. Courtney forced her gaze up past his nose. Considering the heat in his eyes, she wondered how her clothing wasn't on fire.

The arms around her kept her from moving away. Exactly when he'd put them around her, she didn't know, but she wasn't in any rush for him to move them either. Unfortunately, they were getting in the way of other skaters. Already a small group forced to go around had thrown dirty looks in their direction.

"I'm ready for a break." She unclasped her hands from behind his neck and settled her palms back on his shoulders. "Why don't we go to Ambrosia for some hot chocolate? After, we can stop in Benoit Jewelers and look at wedding rings." Benoit wasn't the only jewelry store in the city, but in her opinion, its selection far surpassed any other in Providence.

He loosened his embrace, but his arms remained where they were. "Whatever you want."

Talk about a loaded response. Part of her wanted to say "let's go home and spend the rest of the afternoon getting reacquainted with each other's bodies." Her more logical side reminded her why it was a good idea to keep their relationship as platonic as possible and urged her to remain in public places.

The left side of her brain switched back on. "We still need wedding rings. We might as well get them today."

NINE

Josh grabbed the cell phone on the nightstand and checked the caller ID. The device had remained silent up until now, unlike Courtney's. He'd lost count of how many calls she'd received between the time they left the ice rink and returned to the Mayfair. Several of the calls she'd ignored. The handful she took were short, and she'd ended each of them with the promise to call whoever it was back later.

Mom appeared on his screen now. Despite the text message she'd sent him earlier in the week and the media attention since news of their engagement went public, she hadn't called him back. Even though Josh hadn't met the woman yet, he knew if Marilyn Belmont had received a similar message to the one he left, she would've been on Courtney's doorstep within a matter of hours.

He considered letting the call go to voice mail. So far, his day had been fantastic. He knew from experience a conversation with his mom could easily ruin it. Josh didn't think she set out to do that, but rather she simply didn't always think before she spoke. Most of the time she was too concerned about herself and what was going on in her little world to think about anyone else, including her three children—a fact he and his siblings accepted a long time ago.

Still, it was his mother. She deserved to know the details of his upcoming wedding. Whether or not she attended was up to her.

He pressed the green icon before the device rang again. "Hey, Mom."

"When I got your message, I thought it was some kind of practical joke," she said after greeting him.

Pinching the bridge of his nose, Josh shook his head. A practical joke? When had he ever been known to pull practical jokes? And if he did decide to take it up, he wouldn't have started by telling his mother he was engaged.

"But then Eve mentioned it when she stopped by on Wednesday night."

He'd met Eve, his mom's stepdaughter, once, and it'd been when his mom married Trevor six years ago. It didn't surprise him she'd mentioned his engagement. While he didn't interact with the woman, his sister, Shannon, did. According to her, when Eve wasn't promoting her new fashion line, she was either posting pictures of herself in various states of undress or searching for any mention of herself in the media.

"I saw the pictures of you and Courtney on the *Star Report* website. She is definitely not as beautiful as her sister or her cousin Sara. But she's pretty in a girl-next-door sort of way."

Josh ground his teeth together rather than say what he was thinking, because after all, this was his mother on the phone. He kept his mouth closed until he was confident he could speak and not be rude.

"I disagree, Mom." At least he disagreed with his mom's assessment that her sister and cousin were more attractive. She wasn't far off by saying Courtney had that girl-next-door look. Although in his head, she had more of a sexy librarian vibe going on.

"We both know what she looks like doesn't matter as much as who she's related to anyway. An association with the Sherbrooke family is going to be great for you," his mom said, further demonstrating that there was no filter between her brain and her mouth.

He considered disconnecting the call. Once again, the fact the woman had given birth to him kept him from doing so. "Mom, I didn't ask her to marry me because of who she's related to." If the dull ache in his forehead was any indication, the sooner he ended this call the better.

Evidently, even his tone-deaf mother didn't miss the anger in his voice, because after a moment she said, "Josh, of course, I wasn't saying you did. But it must have occurred to you how beneficial being a part of that family will be."

His mom didn't give him a chance to disagree before continuing. "I read the wedding is on the first in Newport."

At the knock on the bedroom door, Josh crossed the room and opened the door. "Yeah, we decided against a long engagement." He gestured for Courtney to enter. "I know it is short notice, so if you and Trevor can't make it, I understand."

Left up to him, she wouldn't come, but he'd never tell her that. Besides, not only was it short notice, but the wedding was taking place in New England in February. His mom hated the cold. One of the first things she'd done after divorcing his dad was move out to the West Coast.

"I wouldn't miss it. I'm not sure about Trevor's schedule, but I'll be there."

Damn it. "Great. I look forward to seeing you." *You're playing a role,* Josh reminded himself. He glanced in Courtney's direction. At the moment, her back was to him as she looked out the floor-to-ceiling windows. "Courtney and I have plans tonight, so I need to go, but I'll text you the details."

No way was he telling her their plans involved him meeting Courtney's parents. If he shared that detail, she might offer to arrive a day or two before the wedding so she could get to know Courtney. His mom in the same room with Courtney and her family was one thing. During the wedding and reception, there wouldn't be too much opportunity for the two of them to speak. If his mom visited them here, she would have Courtney's full attention, and there was no predicting what comments she might make.

At the sound of her name, Courtney turned and shook her head. "No rush," she whispered. He ignored her.

After disconnecting the call, Josh shoved the device in his pocket and rubbed the area above his left eyebrow. Most people didn't get a headache from talking to their mothers. Then again, when it came to mothers, Scarlett Basto was one of a kind.

"You didn't have to cut your conversation short. If we're a few minutes late, it's not a big deal." She slipped her hands into the back pockets of her jeans, something he'd almost done himself when she'd kissed him on the ice. The fear she'd pull her sweet mouth away from his if he did had kept his palms pressed against her back.

Yeah, I did. "Mom and I were done."

The wisest course of action would be to insist they leave before he lost the battle and decided getting her mouth against his again was more important than letting her control the pace of their relationship. Making wise decisions wasn't something he was well-known for. Rounding the bed, he closed in on her.

He stopped less than an arm's length away, but she didn't retreat or suggest they leave. "It sounded like she's coming to the wedding." Thanks to the three-inch heels on her boots, they were almost the same height, and she locked her eyes with his.

Another step closer and he could kiss her. How would she react if he did? Would she melt against him as she had earlier, or would she remind him she was only pretending to be in love with him?

"Unfortunately." Distracted by his thoughts and the way her sweater clung to her breasts, the answer slipped out.

Courtney's eyebrows shot up faster than an old-fashioned jack in the box. "Unfortunately? You don't want your mother there?"

And he complained his mom didn't have a filter between her mouth and brain. Maybe he didn't either. "Mom seeks attention everywhere she goes. The fact it's our wedding won't matter to her." No point in sugarcoating the truth. It was better Courtney knew what to expect before she met his mom.

A smile tugged at the corners of her mouth as she tucked some hair behind her right ear. "I've seen articles referring to your mom as a diva. Sounds like for once the media wasn't exaggerating."

"Diva, yeah, that's one word you could use to describe her." Reaching out, he tucked the hair on the other side of her face behind her left ear. "All eyes should be on you that day. Not her." He gave his fingers permission to skim across her jaw and down her neck. Rather than push his hand away or tell him to stop, she moved closer and settled a hand on his waist.

The feel of her hand against his body caused him to lose the battle. Lowering his mouth to hers, Josh anchored her against him with his arms. Tenderly he brushed his lips back and forth against hers, urging her to open for him. When she did, her tongue tangled with his and lust as well as another emotion he couldn't name broke over him like a wave.

In his head, he envisioned placing her on the bed and then peeling off her sweater and skinny jeans. Before he gave in to the temptation, he pulled his lips away. "Maybe we should go."

If he looked in her face and saw even a hint that she was suffering from the same emotions plaguing him, he'd lose what little self-control he had. So instead he rested his forehead against hers and kept his arms locked around her because he wasn't ready to let her go.

"Probably." Thank God, her voice echoed the battle he was waging. Courtney dropped her arms by her sides and took a step away from him, proving that at least one of them had some common sense left. "I don't want us to be too late."

He'd dated what many considered some of the most beautiful women in the world. As far as he was concerned, none of them compared to the woman standing in front of him. Unlike many of those women, she didn't rely on makeup and plastic surgeons to perfect her looks. She had a natural beauty that no one could artificially replicate. How could his mom think her sister and cousin were prettier?

———

BY THE TIME they turned into her parents' driveway, the clock read quarter past five. Courtney hated being late. Today she had no one to blame but herself. She'd only knocked on Josh's door to let him know she was ready to go whenever he was. When she'd seen he was on the phone, she should've turned around and walked back into the kitchen or just about any other part of the penthouse and waited for him. But had she done that? Nope.

Instead, she'd entered his bedroom, the one room in the house that should be off-limits to her. For someone with an IQ of 154, she'd been doing some pretty questionable things over the past couple of months.

Even with her first misstep, they would've made it to her parents by five if she'd moved closer to the door rather than Josh when he skimmed his fingers across her jaw. Once he'd done it, she'd been a goner. The current time and getting to her parents' became the farthest thing from her mind. All she could concentrate on was the way he looked at her—like she was the most important person in the world. She'd read somewhere a person's eyes could tell you what they truly felt. While she believed that might be true for some, she wasn't sure it pertained to an individual whose career demanded they constantly portray emotions they didn't feel.

The Tudor-style mansion came into view as the car rounded the corner, and she groaned when she noticed the three vehicles parked out front. After her mom mentioned inviting her aunts and uncles, she'd kept her fingers crossed they wouldn't come and it would only be her parents, brother, sister, and Paige tonight. The black SUV with Virginia plates in front of them told her not only had her mom invited her aunts and uncles, but she'd invited her cousins too. And if Jake was here, who else might be on their way?

Courtney held Josh's hand as they walked up the front steps. Tonight wasn't only about her family meeting Josh, it was also about selling the story that they were very much in love and had been for months.

"Looks like my uncle Mark and my cousin Jake are here." She pressed the doorbell. Normally she'd let herself in, but since Josh drove tonight, she'd left her keys at home. "I'm not sure who the third car belongs to. It might be Uncle Jonathan's." The silver Bentley with Massachusetts license plates was something he would drive, but if it belonged to him, she'd never seen it.

The door opened before either of them could say anything else, and Marilyn Belmont greeted them. "I was starting to worry," she said, allowing them to enter. "You usually call when you're running late."

Actually, it was more like she never ran late, but she wouldn't contradict her mom. "I'm sorry. It took me a little longer than I expected to get ready." Courtney hugged her mom and then slipped off her jacket. A formal introduction was unnecessary for several reasons, yet she felt the need to say something. Her mom beat her to it.

"I've been looking forward to meeting you all week, Josh." Her mom smiled and not surprisingly hugged Josh. He didn't hesitate to return the embrace. He even dropped a polite kiss on Marilyn's cheek.

"Courtney has told me a lot about you and her father, Mrs. Belmont."

"You're about to be family. Please call me Marilyn," her mom said, touching his shoulder. "I'm going to see how dinner is coming along," she continued. "Your sister went upstairs to take a call, but everyone else is in the living room. I'll meet you in there."

For private family gatherings, her parents preferred to use the smaller living room situated near the back of the house. When she paused in the doorway, she found her dad, Uncle Mark, and Uncle Jonathan seated in a small circle, more than likely discussing politics. Her sister-in-law, her cousin Jake, and his wife sat with Abby, her uncle Mark's third wife, and Courtney's aunt Judith, while Scott sat on the floor playing with his son.

Earlier in the week, she'd spoken with her dad. Tuesday night, not long after she arrived home, he called to offer his congratulations. Much like her mom, he'd questioned her decision to marry so soon. Then he'd gone on to offer his advice—advice that had included getting a prenup, something she already had an attorney working on, and thinking twice before marrying an actor. He wouldn't bring up the matter with Josh there, but if they found themselves alone, he wouldn't hesitate to again suggest she postpone the wedding. Although she recognized her dad only had her best interests in mind, his comments rubbed her the wrong way.

"What's wrong?" Josh whispered, his breath warm against her skin.

Wrong? Nothing, except she needed to introduce Josh to her dad, and judging by the comments he'd made on the phone, he had already formed an opinion of him—an opinion that was anything but complimentary.

"Honestly, I'm a little nervous." Josh was on the shortlist of people she could be honest with these days—a situation she didn't at all care for.

She kept hold of his hand as she walked toward her dad, partially because it helped sell the act, but also because she simply liked the physical contact.

Dad won't say anything with Josh standing there.

If Harrison Belmont was anything, it was proper and polite. Actually, both her parents were. In fact, she couldn't remember a time when either of her parents had done something that embarrassed her, which was something most of her friends couldn't say about their parents.

Her dad stood and met them before they reached the group. "Your mom was getting worried about you." Harrison put his arms around her and kissed her cheek. "Did you hit a lot of traffic?"

Shaking her head, she returned the hug before stepping back. "We just got a late start." Courtney put her arm around Josh's waist. "Dad, this is Josh."

Extending his hand in Josh's direction, her dad offered up a tight smile. "It's nice to meet you." He gestured toward where he'd been sitting and clapped Josh on the shoulder. "Let me introduce you to Courtney's uncles."

Talk about being brought into the lion's den. The way she saw it, Josh had no choice but to follow her dad, and she had no intention of sending him in alone.

By the time Josh finished shaking hands with her two uncles, Juliette had entered the room. No matter the time or place, her sister always looked as if she'd just come from one of her photo shoots. Tonight wasn't any different.

"Arriving late. You really are becoming more like me," her sister said as she hugged her. Unlike everyone else so far, when Juliette smiled at Josh it was genuine. "We met last year at one of Seth Vallencourt's parties. It's nice to see you again."

Josh returned her sister's embrace. "I remember, I was with...."

He didn't need to finish his sentence. Thanks to her conversation with Juliette earlier this week, Courtney already knew whom he'd been with. A bowling ball settled in her stomach as she remembered how Juliette had said Selena Cruise had been draped all over Josh that night.

Who he'd been with before they met didn't matter. At least, it shouldn't matter, especially since they weren't getting married for love. The evil green-eyed monster didn't seem to realize that fact.

"I'm sorry I was gone so long. Your aunt Elizabeth called. She said she tried calling you earlier today but got your voice mail," Mom said, entering the room and joining them.

Thanks a lot, Mom. Her lousy timing had saved Josh from finishing his sentence. While the party had happened months before they met, Courtney wondered if he would've been honest about whom had he been with that night.

"She asked me to pass along her and Warren's congratulations. She wants you to call her when you have a chance," her mom continued before turning her attention to the room as a whole. "Dinner will be ready in a few minutes."

Before her mom could bring up the wedding or any other questions she didn't want to answer right now, Courtney grabbed Josh's hand and led him over to where the rest of the family was gathered. The move would only postpone her mom's comments, but for now, she'd take what she could get.

Again, formal introductions seemed unnecessary. Even if they'd never seen any of Josh's movies, the chances of her family members never seeing a picture of him somewhere was slim. Still, she did what her manners dictated and introduced Josh first to her aunt Judith and then to Abby, Uncle Mark's third wife, a woman she'd known long before she married into the family nine years ago. She and Donna Sherbrooke, her uncle Mark's first wife and her dad's sister, had been best friends for years. Even after Aunt Donna's death almost twenty years ago, Abby had remained close to the family. Once she'd introduced Josh to the women of the group, she moved on to perhaps her favorite person there.

"This gorgeous guy is Cooper," she said, scooping up her nephew. Settling him on her hip, she kissed his forehead and again wondered how it was possible Cooper was already over a year old and walking. It truly seemed like just the other day she'd held him while making sure to support his tiny head.

"I guess it's a good thing we've met," Scott said, extending his hand toward Josh. "It's nice to see you again."

Annoying her older brother was one of those things she'd loved doing when they were younger and something she had never fully outgrown. These days she didn't get much of an opportunity, since he spent most of his time in New York. "Hey, I was getting to you. Some people are simply more important though. Right, Cooper?" Cooper giggled when she tickled him.

She glanced away from her nephew as her brother's words sank in. "You've met?" Trent and Josh were friends. They had been for years. Considering Trent's lifestyle before he met his wife, it didn't surprise her. But her brother had never been anything like Trent.

"When I was with Nicole, we attended a few of the same parties as Josh," Scott replied.

She resisted the urge to roll her eyes at the mention of Nicole Sutton, Cooper's mother. Scott had dated the actress for several months long before he met his wife. Even before Scott ended their relationship because he found out she was cheating on him, Courtney hadn't cared for the woman or understood why her brother was wasting his time with her. Her opinion of Nicole only deteriorated more after she leaned Nicole had waited until after Cooper was born to tell Scott he might be the father. Since she'd been sleeping with two other men while with Scott, it had taken a paternity test to identify whom Cooper belonged to. While she might be able to forgive the woman for cheating, she couldn't forgive her for hiding the truth about Cooper for so long. Especially since Scott was a fantastic father. There wasn't anything her brother wouldn't do for his son. And when Paige gave birth later in the year, the same would be true for those children. Considering the lengths Josh was going to to make sure he retained joint custody of his daughter, Josh shared the same trait.

Children. She smiled at the image of her brother trying to handle twins, and she was glad Scott was the one expecting twins and not her. If and when she had children, she wanted them to come one at a time and preferably a few years apart.

"Care to share what's so amusing?" Scott asked.

She considered his question or at least made it look as if she was considering it. "No, not really. But I do think it's time to eat." Across the room, her father and uncles stood as her mom headed their way.

As if he did it every day, Josh's arm went around her waist after she handed Cooper back to Scott. Before she could think about her motives, she leaned into him.

"What was so funny?" His voice remained low.

She slowed her pace so everyone else could pass by them. "Scott and Paige are expecting twins. I was picturing my always-in-control brother trying to handle two babies."

"Twins. Ouch. Better him than me. Taking care of Adalynn after she was born was exhausting enough."

The same sadness she'd heard earlier in the week when he mentioned his daughter resonated in his tone and pulled at her heart. And now, like before, she wanted to hunt down his ex-girlfriend and tell her what a bitch she was being. She understood wanting what was best for your child, and in some cases that meant limiting how much influence a parent would have on a son or daughter. As far as she was concerned, that wasn't necessary in this situation, and she'd do whatever she could to help Josh.

TEN

WHEN IT CAME TO PREPARING MEALS, NOT MANY PEOPLE did it better than her parents' chef, Paulette. The woman could take a piece of toast and turn it into a masterpiece of flavor. The meal served tonight was nothing short of perfection. In fact, it had Courtney thinking she should visit more often, specifically around dinnertime. As for the dessert, well, there weren't words to describe it, and if there was any left in the kitchen, she might take some home with her.

"Where are you going on your honeymoon?" Charlie, Jake's wife, asked. With dinner over, the whole family except for Uncle Jonathan, who'd received a call from her cousin, was once again gathered in the living room.

Beats me. Considering the detailed storyline they'd devised, you would have thought the topic of a honeymoon would've come up at some point. Somehow though it'd slipped both their minds.

Josh gently squeezed her leg, and she took that as a signal to leave the answer to him. "Courtney doesn't want to take time off from the foundation right now, so we decided to wait and go somewhere this summer."

Well, he wasn't wrong. She'd only been with the Helping Hands Foundation since the middle of December. It was a little too soon to be taking a vacation. But at some point they'd need to go on a honeymoon, so it was a topic they'd need to discuss later.

"If you postponed the wedding by six or seven months, taking a few weeks off wouldn't be an issue," her mom said.

She'd expected her mom to mention changing the date long before now. The fact she'd made it until after dessert without mentioning it was amazing.

"And then you could have everything outside at Cliff House." Now that Mom had started, she wasn't ready to give up. "We could plan something similar to Gray and Kiera's wedding. The winter isn't a good time to get married. You never know what the weather will be."

She couldn't deny her cousin Gray's wedding back in June had been gorgeous and romantic. Under different circumstances, she wouldn't mind something similar, but time wasn't on their side. And as far as the season went, her cousin Trent had gotten married in January and everything had run smoothly.

"Trent and Addie got married in January without any problems." Perhaps a little childish, but she couldn't help remind her mom of that fact. "Besides, the weather can cause problems in the summer too. We all thought Gray and Kiera would have to move everything inside, remember?"

For days leading up to her cousin's wedding, the family kept their fingers crossed that the storm moving up across the Atlantic would stall or change course.

"When it comes to planning something like a wedding, every season has its drawbacks," Aunt Judith added. "Jonathan and I got married in September, and a nor'easter hit two days before the wedding."

Courtney wasn't a meteorologist, but she knew most

nor'easters tended to occur sometime between late fall and early spring, but they could happen at other times as well. Later, she'd have to thank her aunt for pointing out how unpredictable the weather could be regardless of the time of the year.

Marilyn pinched her lips together and reached for her tea without commenting.

"I think we should just be happy they're inviting us to the wedding, unlike someone else in this room that we know and love," Juliette said, looking everywhere but at Jake and Charlie.

She hadn't been surprised when the couple had a secret wedding without his parents or the majority of the family in attendance. Her cousin Jake liked to do things his own way. Courtney suspected no one in the family had really been shocked when they found out either, including his parents.

"Hey, I recommend doing it our way. If the media doesn't know it's about to happen, they can't get in the way." For the most part, the only time he landed in the news these days was when it pertained to his disaster relief organization. However, before he met and married Charlie, the media had constantly hounded him.

Josh moved his hand off her leg and put his arm around her shoulders. "I suggested we elope," he said before kissing her temple. "But Courtney was against it. She wanted her family there."

He's definitely playing the part tonight. When he wasn't touching her hand, he was putting an arm around her, and forget about the way he looked at her. Occasionally, she almost forgot their relationship wasn't real.

Reaching up, she caressed his fingers resting on her shoulder. "The media won't get past the gates at Cliff House, so I'm not worried about them bothering us. And if Uncle Warren or

Aunt Elizabeth make it, there will be Secret Service all around too."

Usually, she considered the extra security a downside to having an uncle who also happened to be the President of the United States. In this instance, it might prove to be beneficial.

"I know Mom and Dad plan to attend Leah's wedding." Jake pulled his ringing cell phone from his pocket and glanced at the screen. "It's Sean."

Conversation stopped while he greeted his brother-in-law. Earlier in the evening, Jake had mentioned Sean and Mia were watching his and Charlie's son, Garrett, tonight. Other than to let Jake and Charlie know their son was sick, she couldn't think of a good reason he'd be calling.

"Thanks for the heads-up. I'll talk to Charlie and see what she wants to do and get back to you."

"Is everything okay?" Charlie asked before Jake could share any details.

"Sean wanted to let us know the roads are already nasty and there is a multicar accident on 128. He suggested we stay here tonight."

She hadn't thought about the weather or paid any attention to what was going on outside since they arrived. The snow wasn't supposed to start for a few more hours, giving them more than enough time to get home before road conditions deteriorated. But she should've. She'd lived in New England all her life and knew how quickly the weather could change. Given the time of night, she wasn't likely to see much, but she looked toward the windows anyway.

"If it's snowing, I'd feel better if you and Charlie stayed," Marilyn said before glancing in Courtney's direction. "The same goes for you and Josh. You have an even longer drive home."

On the rare occasion she spent the night, she stayed in her

old bedroom. But stay here tonight? With Josh. In the same room. It might be safer to brave the nasty roads.

Jake didn't hesitate to accept her mom's invitation. "I'll call Sean back and let him know we'll be back in the morning."

"What about you two?" her mom asked, looking first at Courtney and then Josh.

"Whatever Courtney wants is fine with me," Josh answered, leaving the ball squarely in her court.

Jeopardizing their safety so they didn't have to share a bedroom made no sense whatsoever. "I guess it might be better if we stay too."

With her question answered, Marilyn turned her attention toward her brother Mark and Abby. They were the only other people in the room who had more than a five-minute drive ahead of them, since Jonathan and his wife lived in the same neighborhood.

If they stayed down here visiting long enough, perhaps she'd be so exhausted by the time they went upstairs that she'd fall asleep immediately and not even notice Josh was in the same room. *One can hope.*

"Courtney and Charlie, I should have something you can sleep in," Juliette said.

She didn't doubt it. Although her sister had an apartment in New York City, she spent a lot of time here, and her closet upstairs proved it.

COURTNEY SNUGGLED into Josh's side while her parents finished saying goodnight to the occupants in the room. While Uncle Jonathan and his wife had left shortly after Jake's phone call, Uncle Mark and Abby had decided to stay the night. They'd retired upstairs at least a half an hour ago. Paige, who'd been struggling to keep her eyes open, had followed not long after them.

"I don't have much time to plan a bachelorette party." Juliette waited until their mother left the room before bringing up the topic. Courtney didn't think it was a coincidence either. Following Jake's phone call, the conversation moved away from Courtney's wedding. The mention of a bachelorette party would only bring it back to the forefront of their mom's thoughts and thus back to the center of their conversation. Her sister knew she'd prefer it if everyone's attention was focused on something else.

"I know you didn't have one, but do you have any ideas, Charlie?" Juliette asked.

"We took my sister-in-law to play laser tag for her bachelorette party," Charlie answered. "When my friend Jessie got married, we went into Boston for a show and dinner."

Not surprisingly, Juliette made a face at the suggestions. She found theatrical productions boring. As for laser tag, she might break a nail.

"No bachelorette party," Courtney said before her sister could get invested in the idea.

Many of the people she'd want there didn't live locally. No way did she want her family members coming to the area for a bachelorette party and then again taking time out of their schedules to travel here so they could help celebrate a temporary wedding.

"C'mon. It'll be fun. We can keep it small and do it the weekend before the wedding," her sister said. "I'm sure Evan is throwing Josh a bachelor party."

Josh's brother knew the truth about their upcoming wedding, but it didn't mean he wouldn't throw Josh one hell of a party. More than likely it'd be at some so-called gentlemen's club in Manhattan where he'd be surrounded by beautiful barely dressed women—women who'd be more than happy to give Josh all the extra attention he wanted, both inside and outside the club.

"Is Evan throwing you one?" Could she sound any more like a jealous shrew? Probably not.

"No. I told him I didn't want one."

Or he's not bothering because he knows the truth about the wedding. Either way, relief flared in her chest. Once they went their separate ways, Josh might spend his free nights with naked women, but for now, he'd be hanging out at her place watching old black-and-white sitcoms.

"Oh." Her sister appeared to be having a difficult time accepting Josh's answer. "All my friends have had them. Why don't you want one?" Juliette asked.

"Maybe I'd say yes if there was more time, but it's silly to have you and everyone else visit two weekends in a row." *Next time I get married, you can throw me a party.*

Josh sipped his scotch and tried to pay attention as Jake described the relief efforts his foundation was still conducting in Puerto Rico following the devastating hurricane they'd experienced months ago. He'd heard of the Falmouth Foundation, but he assumed Jake spent his time running it from the comfort of his office in Virginia. By the sound of it though, Jake spent a lot of time on the ground doing whatever needed to be done.

"Charlie and Garrett are staying up in North Salem and visiting while I head down there for a few days," Jake said, reaching for the bottle of scotch and adding a splash more to his glass.

Evidently Jake hadn't traveled up from Virginia because Courtney's mom invited him. Rather, he'd already been in the state to visit his wife's family. When he learned Scott was in the area with his family, he'd made plans to see them. Those plans had simply coincided with tonight's dinner, so Scott had invited Jake and his wife to join them.

"Anyone else?" Jake asked rather than set the bottle down.

He'd been nursing his drink since Scott handed it to him. In general, straight scotch wasn't his favorite. He would have preferred more of the wine they'd enjoyed while the women were still with the group, but he accepted the drink after Courtney went upstairs anyway. It gave him an excuse to stay behind while she got settled into bed and possibly fell asleep—something he doubted he'd be doing tonight with her in the same room.

Unless necessary, it was irresponsible to drive during a snowstorm. It put not only yourself in danger but also any people around you. As far as their physical safety was concerned, Courtney had made the right decision. Unfortunately, the same couldn't be said when it came to his mental well-being. He'd been unable to keep his hands off her while in a room surrounded by her family. How the hell was he going to manage it when they were not only alone but had a nice comfy bed at their disposal? Yeah, no way was he falling asleep tonight.

He'd thought sleeping down the hall from her all week was torture. The night ahead of him promised to be so much worse.

"All set." Josh took the last mouthful of liquid.

"No thanks. I'm heading up," Scott answered as he stood.

Jake tossed back his drink and added his glass to the empty wineglasses on the table. "Probably not a bad idea."

Too bad Josh didn't have anything left in his glass. He could stay behind to finish it and maybe spend the night on the sofa. If he set the alarm on his phone, he might have been able to wake up before anyone discovered him there.

With that option off the table, Josh followed the men up the central staircase. At the top, two hallways branched off.

"See you both in the morning," Jake said before he headed down the hallway on the left.

"Courtney's room is across from mine," Scott said, turning to the right. He stopped halfway down the hall and reached for a doorknob. "Goodnight."

Not a sound came from the other side of Courtney's door. She had gone up well over an hour ago, giving her more than enough time to change and fall asleep. If he could help it, he'd prefer not to wake her up when he went inside.

The door opened without so much as a squeak, and he gently closed it behind him. She'd left the light on in what he guessed was the bathroom. Although the door was partially closed, it allowed just enough light in the room for him to make out the furniture and avoid walking into anything. He'd hoped there might be a recliner or a sofa in the room that he could use as a bed. No such luck though.

He considered the armchair over by the windows. Judging by the looks of it, the bathtub would be a more comfortable place to sleep. With the chair out, he had only two other options: the bed or the floor.

It won't kill me to sleep on the floor. He couldn't say the same about the bed.

She left the comforter folded at the end of the bed. It'd make a decent sleeping bag for the night. Josh kicked off his shoes, then removed his shirt and pants. If he had to wear them again in the morning, he'd rather they not look like he slept in them. After grabbing the comforter, he reached for a pillow.

The shape in the bed moved, and a second later a bedside light switched on. "You don't have to sleep on the floor." Propped up on an elbow, she didn't look like someone who had been asleep for an hour.

"Are you sure?"

She nodded and flipped back the blankets so he could get under them.

Bad idea. Very bad idea. The warning flashed like a neon sign in his head. Ignoring it, he climbed into bed.

Fifteen minutes later, Josh stared into the darkness, every cell in his body accurately aware of just who was in the king-size bed with him. He could reach out and touch her. Cover her lips with his while he palmed her breasts and teased her nipples. Once finished with her mouth, he could move his lips down her body and pleasure her like he had so many times in Hawaii before slipping inside her so they could climax together. If he were lucky, she'd wake him up in the morning with some similar treatment.

He groaned at the images conjured up by his mind. He should've stuck with his plan and slept on the floor. Would the discomfort of being on the floor have been any better than what he was currently experiencing?

No, it would've been worse. Not only would he have been suffering from a hard-on, but he would've also had a sore back. At least in bed, his back wasn't bothering him.

The sheets covering his body moved as the mattress shifted slightly and bare skin brushed against his thigh.

Great, just what he needed. Already he was hugging the edge of the mattress. If he moved over any further, he would be on the floor. He had two choices, either wake her and ask her to move or suck it up and hope she rolled back to where she'd been. Both options sucked.

Fingertips touched his chest. During their two weeks together, he'd often woken up and found her arm across his body or a leg pressed against his. Back then, he'd enjoyed it. Tonight, her heat burned into his chest and caused every muscle in his body to tighten.

Closing his eyes, Josh focused on his breathing instead of the lithe, warm body pressed against his side. He didn't recall much from the meditation classes he'd attended, but he remembered he was supposed to do that.

One. Two. Thre— A gentle kiss landed on his shoulder, sending Josh's count out the window. Another one quickly followed, and he stopped breathing too.

With each kiss, she got closer to his neck. At the same time, the hand on his chest moved lower. When it passed over his abdomen, his muscles clenched.

Please don't stop. Countless times in Hawaii, she'd woken him up this way.

Her hand paused at the waistband of his underwear, sending his heart rate off the charts. Before he could say or do anything, it slipped beneath the fabric and closed around him.

Whatever blood was left in his brain skyrocketed south. With a groan, he grabbed the sheet beneath him and he forced himself to let her pleasure him without touching her. When her mouth came down on his, he snapped. No longer able to keep his hands to himself, he rolled onto his side and slipped them under her top.

MOVING ONTO HER BACK, Courtney pulled up the blanket so it covered both of them. When she'd climbed into bed last night, she'd truly hoped to be asleep by the time Josh came up. Instead, she'd tossed and turned while thinking about all the ways Josh could pleasure her if she let him. By the time the bedroom door opened, every inch of her body ached for his touch. Still, she might have been able to hold out if she hadn't turned the light on and seen him standing with nothing on but his boxer briefs. Not only had he been standing next to the bed in just his underwear, but he'd been there fully erect.

When they'd been downstairs, he constantly had an arm around her or a hand on her leg. After he got into bed, she waited for him to pull her close, giving her the okay to touch him. It never happened. Instead, Josh stayed as close to the edge of the bed as possible, reinforcing his statement on Monday that he'd let her decide if they had sex.

Before she lost her nerve, Courtney let him know she'd made up her mind. And at some point today, she planned to remind him of her decision.

Josh's leg rubbed against hers as he moved. A moment later, he draped an arm across her. "Morning." He kissed her bare shoulder and sent a jolt of energy straight to her nipple. "How did you sleep?" The hand on her stomach inched up, and Josh's thumb brushed the underside of her breast.

They hadn't done much sleeping last night. "Not bad. You?"

"Best sleep I've had since I came back from vacation." Kissing the pulse in her neck, he teased her taut nipple with his fingers.

Thanks to the sunlight sneaking into the room, she knew it was morning. Just how early, she didn't know. She'd like a chance to say goodbye before her family members left. If they continued down the path they were on, it was possible everyone would be gone by the time they got downstairs. So before it became impossible for her to form a coherent thought, she should get up and put some clothes on. Besides, it wasn't like they couldn't spend the rest of the day naked in her bedroom at home.

"Josh."

"What?" He cupped her breast and touched the tip of his tongue to her nipple.

"We...." His lips closed around her nipple, sending her thoughts up in a puff of smoke.

To hell with it. Taking his hand, she guided it down her body and to the spot aching the most for his touch. If her family left before they made an appearance, she'd see everyone in a few weeks anyway.

ELEVEN

Courtney looked over the spread on the kitchen island and ran through her mental list. Crackers, check. Cheese and dip, yep, those were out too, along with tortilla chips and pepper slices. She'd wait to take any wine out, and Josh was picking up beer and should be home soon. And the boneless chicken wings were in the oven. So why did it feel like she was forgetting something?

From behind her, Josh put his arms around her waist, letting her know he'd returned. "How soon will Trent and Addie be here?" He kissed her neck, momentarily distracting her.

When she'd canceled her plans with her cousin and his wife, she'd invited them over tonight instead for game night. Usually, either Trent or her cousin Gray hosted game night, and more often than not they played a board game like Telestrations or Codenames. Occasionally, they'd play cards. Since she didn't own any board games, tonight they'd be playing cards. More specifically they'd be playing Pitch, the only card game other than solitaire that she knew well.

Pepperoni. She'd left it in the refrigerator. "Less than thirty minutes."

Kissing her neck again, he slipped his hands under her sweatshirt. "Then we have a little time." He moved one of the ice blocks masquerading as a hand higher while the other headed toward the button of her jeans.

"Your hands are freezing."

"I'm trying to warm them up." His hand freed one breast from her bra.

Sunday afternoon when they returned from her parents', they'd gone almost immediately from the parking garage to her bedroom. They'd spent the majority of the day in there. During one of their trips into the kitchen for food, she'd invited him to move into her room. Since she'd allowed their relationship to become intimate again, it didn't make a lot of sense for him to sleep in another room, especially since she enjoyed waking up and finding his arm around her at night or falling asleep with her head resting on his shoulder. He'd agreed immediately. They'd had sex every night and almost every morning since, including this morning.

The hand heading south undid the button and slipped lower. Like his other hand, it remained cold from being outside, and the contrast in temperatures between his skin and hers sent all the nerve endings in her body on overload.

If she let him continue, they'd end up naked in her bed or maybe the sofa. Perhaps they wouldn't even get that far. Last night they hadn't made it out of the kitchen. Wherever they ended up, she didn't want to be in the middle of having sex when her cousin and Addie arrived. Already she expected Trent to give her a hard time tonight. She didn't need to keep him waiting and then answer the door with her hair a mess and her sweatshirt on backward because she'd been in such a rush to get dressed.

"Have you thought about wearing gloves?"

His hand moved lower, and he ran his finger over the spot silently begging for his touch. "Why would I do that when I have you at home?"

She bit down on her lip to keep from moaning. "Josh, we really don't have a lot of time." But oh man, she wished they did.

"Are you sure?" He moved his fingers against her again while his hand freed her other breast from her bra, nearly sending her right over the edge.

Maybe if we're really quick. Reaching behind herself, she slipped the button on his jeans free.

The doorbell stopped her from doing anything else. Her cousin's timing sucked.

"If we don't answer, maybe they'll go away," Josh suggested. Both his body and his hands remained where they were.

Taking hold of his wrists, she moved his hands away. "Addie knows I'm home. She sent me a text not long before you got here. Trent will ring the bell until we answer."

As if to prove her point, the doorbell chimed again.

After fixing her bra and buttoning her jeans, she turned. "Smile. It's not like they're staying the night."

Courtney took her own advice and pasted on a smile before opening the door.

"Took you long enough," Trent greeted, giving her a hug and a kiss on the cheek when he walked in. "If we interrupted you, we can entertain ourselves until you're done." His grin said what his words didn't.

Heat rushed to her face. Josh should've answered the door.

Addie elbowed Trent in the side. "Ignore him. He's cranky. He got home late and didn't get to eat before we left."

"We've got plenty of snacks. Josh bought some beer too." She accepted their jackets and hung them in the closet. "Everything is in the kitchen."

Her cousin's expression grew serious. "I'd like to talk to you," Trent said, and Addie shook her head at him.

"C'mon, Trent, we talked about this. Let's just play cards."

Addie didn't need to say any more. "It's okay, Addie. I know what he wants." Courtney also knew Trent wouldn't let the matter go. If they didn't have the discussion now, he'd find another time for them to have it. "Josh is in the kitchen. Can you go over the rules again with him? He's never played Pitch before. We'll be right in."

Addie nodded. "But if Trent says something you don't like, tell me. I'll make sure he pays for it later."

For this conversation, much like the one with Scott on Saturday, she wanted some privacy. "Follow me."

She didn't spend a lot of time in the home office. Today though, a few things had come up after she left the foundation, so she'd come in here to work. When she left, she never bothered to switch off the lights or close her laptop.

"Okay. Out with it, so we can play cards." She loved her cousin, but really, she didn't need him butting into her life.

Whether it was to annoy her or because he wasn't sure how to start, Trent sat down rather than answer her. "Are you going to sit?"

"If it means you'll hurry up, I'll stand on my head."

His eyebrow went up, and he ran a hand across his jaw while considered her words. "That I'd like to see."

This was getting her nowhere. And the quicker she sat, the sooner he'd talk. "Okay, I'm sitting. What do you want to tell me?"

"I didn't say anything when those pictures of you and Josh in Hawaii appeared, because I thought the two of you were just having fun on vacation. I didn't know you'd been seeing him since the summer."

Thanks to Addie, she'd already known why Trent never mentioned Josh to her following her trip.

"But are you sure about marrying him? Josh isn't your type."

Wow, this conversation sounded similar to the one between her and Scott Saturday night. "You know better than most you can't believe everything you read about a person."

"I've known him for years, so trust me, I know what parts of his reputation are true and which are not. He's never stayed with anyone long except for Naomi, and he's been with probably as many women as me. When guys like him get married, it rarely lasts."

"Should I be warning Addie then?"

"Hell no. You know that."

"And thanks to you and Jake, I know people can change. So even if he's been with over two hundred women and participated in orgies, it doesn't mean we won't be happy together."

"Damn, I can't argue with you there." Leaning forward, he rested his forearms on his thighs and laced his fingers together. "I just don't want to see you get hurt."

During their private conversation at their parents' house, Scott had said the same thing. And tonight she'd give Trent the same answer she'd given her brother. "It won't happen. No marriage is perfect, but we love each other. We'll be fine."

"Orgies, huh? Yeah, you don't have to worry about that. If he'd ever taken part in one, he would have told me."

JOSH TUCKED an arm behind his head while he waited for Courtney to come to bed. He knew Trent had talked to her. He hadn't been in the room, but he knew the topic of their conversation. Him.

After they returned, he'd waited for Trent to pull him aside too. And when Courtney took Addie to the bedroom to see her wedding dress, he'd expected his friend to jump on the opportunity. And he had.

He'd started with wanting to know why Josh never told him they were together. Before Trent could get any further, Josh took control and assured him that he'd never do anything to make Courtney unhappy.

Even as he said it, he'd known it was true. In a short amount of time, Courtney's happiness had become important to him. Josh then went on to tell Trent how much he loved Courtney, because he knew Trent needed to hear it. But it wasn't a complete lie either. Too many emotions hit him when he thought about Courtney and their current situation. And he had a feeling love would soon be one of them.

"For your first time playing Pitch, you did well." Getting into bed, Courtney snuggled up next to him. "Did Trent interrogate you when Addie and I left?"

"Nah. He only asked why I didn't tell him we were together." Since he hadn't given Trent a chance to ask anything else, it wasn't a lie. "What did Trent want with you?"

"Playing the role of surrogate big brother. I guess he didn't get the memo that Scott already talked to me. They think we're rushing."

He doubted that was the extent of the conversation. But if she didn't want to share more, he wouldn't push.

She leaned up on her elbow. "I told them whether we get married in a few weeks or a few months, it won't change anything."

Yeah, he didn't agree with her there. In a few more months, a lot of things might have changed.

TWELVE

Thursday night, Courtney pulled into her parking spot, glad to see Josh's car parked right next door. In the almost three weeks he'd been living with her, she'd grown accustomed to coming home and him being there. The handful of occasions she'd arrived home before him, the penthouse had seemed empty and too big—things it had never felt before Josh moved in. If living with him for only a few weeks could do that, what would living with him for possibly a year do? Most of the time she tried not to think about it. Every once in a while, the thought snuck up and bit her in the butt. Like it was now.

It wasn't the only thing that popped its head up from time to time. More times than she'd like to admit, her conscience poked her hard. Each time, it hinted that her heart was becoming fully invested in the relationship. Considering the way she'd felt over the weekend, she suspected it might be true.

Per the temporary custody agreement in place, Adalynn stayed with Josh for the weekend every three weeks. The previous Friday, she'd left work early so they could drive to

Brookline to pick Adalynn up and bring her back to Josh's condo in Boston. A condo she'd learned he'd purchased back in April for no other reason than to have a place closer to his daughter after Josh's ex moved in with her boyfriend, a man who became her fiancé right before Thanksgiving.

From the moment they picked her up, it'd been clear father and daughter adored each other. Their first night together, they'd eaten pizza and made ice cream sundaes before playing Candy Land, his daughter's favorite game, not once but twice. When Josh tucked Adalynn into bed, in a room clearly decorated with the little girl in mind, she'd watched from the doorway as he read her a story. Her conscience took the opportunity to stand up, wave, and shout, "You're in deeper than you intended!"

The following morning, Adalynn made the only two requests Josh denied her all weekend. She'd wanted to go skiing, something her mom didn't do. With their visit so limited though, Josh decided against it but promised to take her soon. He'd also put his foot down when Adalynn asked to eat ice cream for breakfast. Instead, they'd enjoyed pancakes and French toast at a nearby restaurant before spending the day at the Boston Children's Museum, followed by the aquarium—two places Courtney had been to as a child, but hadn't visited in years. For much of the day, Adalynn had walked between them holding their hands. To anyone watching them, they would've appeared like a family enjoying a day in the city. At the same time, it pulled at the loose thread that led back to the fact someday she wanted a family like her brother and so many of her cousins had. Later, when she'd been in bed, she convinced herself the feelings had nothing to do with Josh specifically. Rather, they were associated with the fact her brother had recently gotten married and his wife was pregnant.

Her conclusion lost much of its validity late Sunday afternoon after they dropped Adalynn off with her mom. Gone was the smiling Josh, replaced by a sober, less talkative version. In fact, she didn't think he said a word during the ride back to Providence. And more than anything she'd wanted to wrap her arms around him, promise him everything would work out, and then snap her fingers and reinstate the original custody agreement that had been in place since shortly after Adalynn was born. Unable to change anything, she'd done her best to get his mind on something else, if only for a short time, when they got home. Thankfully, as the week progressed, the Josh she'd grown to know slowly returned.

As she approached the entrance to the building, Courtney retrieved her cell phone from her purse. She'd heard it ring while turning onto West Exchange Street. A glance at the screen had confirmed it was Cliff House's long-time chef, Henri Renault. Finalizing the menu for the reception was the last thing she wanted to do tonight, but with the wedding just around the corner, she didn't have much of a choice. All week she'd been dealing with wedding preparations. Every time she got a call pertaining to it, she wished they'd taken Jake's advice and had a secret wedding, because trying to plan one on such short notice wasn't for her.

"Excuse me, Ms. Belmont."

The woman's voice reached her as she redialed Henri's number. Glancing up, she spotted Aimee Trainor, a reporter and the host of the *Star Insider,* a popular entertainment talk show. A photographer stood alongside her as well as a cameraperson, although at the moment the video camera wasn't pointed in her direction. Courtney wasn't surprised to see the two individuals standing with the woman. Aimee loved to use both videos and photos on her show. The woman had been calling the office almost every day since they announced their engagement. Most reporters did almost anything to get a story, but Aimee stepped over lines others wouldn't cross. So while she'd taken calls from Marcy Blake and Daniella Naulta, two reporters for well-known magazines, she'd dodged all of Aimee's calls. Given Aimee's reputation, she should have known the woman would stop at nothing to get a story, even if it meant traveling from Manhattan to Providence and staking out the Mayfair.

Before Henri answered the phone, Courtney disconnected the call. Finalizing the menu would have to wait a little longer.

"Aimee Trainor, we've been playing telephone tag," she said, extending her gloved hand toward Courtney. Phone tag insinuated Courtney had tried calling the television host back, something she had not done. But there was no point in correcting her. "I hoped we could chat," Aimee continued.

Chat. The woman didn't know the meaning of the word. She'd seen a few episodes of the *Star Insider*, and when the woman did an interview, it resembled an interrogation from a police drama.

She eyed the distance between her and the main entrance. If she made a run for it, she'd only draw more attention her way. People on the sidewalk were already slowing down and looking in their direction. Not to mention, Aimee might sneak inside before the door closed behind her.

"Maybe for a few minutes. I don't have a lot of time tonight." She'd seen family members handle the media before. Sometimes if you gave them an inch, they took it and left you alone. Of course, sometimes the reporters took what you gave them and tried to hang you with it. She'd heard Aimee was the hanging type, so she needed to watch every word she said.

Aimee smiled, reminding Courtney of the Cheshire cat from *Alice in Wonderland,* and she immediately regretted her decision. "Don't worry, I won't take a lot of your time. Earlier this evening I caught J.T. on his way in. He mentioned you have some plans this evening."

Just how long had she been hanging around outside?

Whether Josh had something planned for them or not, she'd use his statement to her advantage. "Uh, yeah. We're meeting with the wedding planner this evening." She ignored the stares following them as they entered the building and walked toward one of the small sitting areas in the lobby.

"Do you mind if I record this?" Aimee pulled off her gloves and winter coat as she sat down.

If she said yes, it might appear as though she had something to hide. While she did, Courtney didn't want Aimee to think she did. "Of course not."

Aimee signaled to the woman with the video camera and the photographer to get into position and waited until the camerawoman gave her a thumbs-up. Then she launched into her list of questions saved on her phone, starting with how they'd met and how they'd managed to keep their romance a secret for so long. After blowing through those at a breakneck speed, she moved on to Josh's reputation—a topic Courtney tried to keep far from her thoughts. Sometimes she was more successful than others.

"How do you feel about the fact J.T. has been associated with so many women over the years?"

"It's in his past, so it doesn't bother me. Just like whoever I dated before him doesn't matter to him." Courtney mentally high-fived herself for giving the reporter what she considered the perfect answer.

The woman patted Courtney's arm as if consoling a dear friend. "I doubt you can compare your past with his. He's been photographed more than once with a topless woman on his boat. And he's been rumored to have threesomes. Not to mention, I have it on good authority he cheated on Naomi Tillman, the mother of his daughter, and that was why she ended their relationship."

They'd never gone into specifics about why his relationship with Naomi ended. Still, the idea he'd cheated on her didn't sit right. As for the other rumor, she'd never heard it mentioned anywhere, but it didn't mean it wasn't true.

But whatever the truth, she wasn't going to let Aimee think his past bothered her. "The past is the past. I've seen people change when they fall in love. My cousin Trent is a perfect example of that. And I know Josh loves me."

Okay, she knew he didn't love her, but he did care about her. If their relationship was truly all about getting back custody of his daughter and physical pleasure, he wouldn't hold her during the night. No, he'd enjoy the sex—correction, the mind-blowing sex—and head back down the hall to his bedroom. He wouldn't make sure he was up every morning so he could have coffee with her before she left for work. And he wouldn't sit around at night and watch old sitcoms with her or play chess.

"True, but not all women would feel the same way. J.T.'s lucky to have someone who is so understanding." Pulling a bottle of water from her giant shoulder bag—the thing was so large Courtney wondered what else she might have inside it—she took a sip before continuing. "Other than a date and location, no details about your upcoming wedding have been released. People are understandably curious, especially since you've only been engaged since December. It's even been suggested you're rushing the wedding because you're pregnant. Is it true?"

The heat burning her neck made an instant detour to her face. That rumor was floating around? Maybe she needed to pay closer attention to the tabloids.

"Nope." One thing she could say with certainty was that she and Josh would never be expecting a child. "Since we just want a small wedding, we saw no reason to have a long engagement."

Aimee's expression went from expectant to disappointed. "So it'll only be family members at the wedding."

They'd both included a handful of friends to the guest list, but Courtney saw no reason to share specific details with the reporter. "More or less." She turned over the cell phone in her hand and glanced at the device. "It's later than I realized. I'm sorry I can't chat longer."

Aimee again flashed her bright smile and stood as Courtney did. "Will you be granting any media outlets access to the wedding?"

"We haven't decided." They discussed it and agreed to keep it as private as possible, so only *Today Magazine* would have access to Cliff House for the wedding. Of course, it wouldn't stop other reporters and photographers from camping outside the fence. The woman standing in front of her didn't need to know that either.

She kept her eyes focused on her destination, the elevator, rather than the people still glancing her way. *Thank you*, she thought when the doors opened immediately, allowing her to escape the unwanted attention.

JOSH GLANCED at his watch while he listened to his father again invite them over this weekend. Where was she? She was usually home by now.

"Sorry, this weekend doesn't work," Josh explained for the second time. "How about one night next week? Maybe Evan and Gemma can join us."

He got it. His dad and Laura wanted to meet Courtney before the wedding. But he had other ideas for them this weekend, ideas that didn't include her family or his. Maybe if his dad had called earlier in the week and invited him, he would've been more open to the idea. The night before he planned to take her away for the weekend was just too late.

"I'll call Evan on Monday and see what he has going on next week and then call you." If another couple joined them at dinner, it would take some of the attention off Courtney. "Say hi to Laura and tell her I hope she feels better soon."

The woman needed to stop going on cruises. Last winter, she'd sprained her wrist when she slipped on water near a pool and tried to break her fall. The winter before that, she got food poisoning while on a cruise in the Caribbean. This time she'd turned her ankle walking down the stairs and broke it, forcing them to end their vacation early and return home.

From inside the kitchen, he heard the door open. Josh stepped into the hall as Courtney slipped off her long wool coat, revealing the forest green, knee-length dress underneath. He didn't know what they called the style of the dress, but he did know it hugged her in all the right places. And he wanted nothing more than to ease it off her shoulders and past her breasts so he could give them the attention they deserved. Then he'd tug it the rest of the way down and take her in the hallway.

But what he wanted and what he planned to do existed on two different planets.

For the sake of his sanity, he forced his gaze north of her breasts. "Hey."

"Hey, yourself." After pulling out the clip holding her hair up, she ran her fingers through it.

He'd seen various emotions on her face. But the agitation there now was a first. "Rough day?"

"It was fine until Aimee Trainor approached me outside. Next time you know there is a reporter hanging around, please give me a heads-up."

She'd cornered him earlier too. He'd thought after their impromptu interview she'd be satisfied and leave because, although not frigid, it was rather cold to stand outside and wait for Courtney to show up. "Sorry, I thought she'd be gone before you got home. You could have blown her off." He rarely ignored a reporter or a fan but only because he didn't want to be labeled an ass. Courtney didn't have to worry about her reputation in the same way.

"She's called my office almost every day since our engagement went public. It seemed easier to answer some questions so she'd stop." She rolled her head from side to side as she kicked off her heels. "Unless you really want to go out, I'd rather stay in tonight." She started to massage the area just behind her left shoulder.

Last night they'd met Evan and his girlfriend for dinner. The night before that, they'd visited her cousin Gray and his wife. Monday, he'd spent much of the evening alone while Courtney spent time with her friend Meg, the same woman he'd shared an elevator with the night he moved in.

Pulling her hand away, Josh kneaded the small knot in her shoulder. "No desire to go out."

"Good. Then I'm changing, and I need to call Henri back. He called me earlier."

"Meet me in the family room when you're done." Since she didn't move away, he continued his massage and started to rub her other shoulder as well.

Courtney's eyes drifted closed. "Mmm."

"I thought you wanted to change."

"To do that, I have to walk away from this," she answered without opening her eyes.

The moment Josh removed his hands and stepped back, Courtney's eyes opened, and she pouted. "Go. Later, I'll finish the massage."

"You better."

"Scout's honor."

She poked him gently. "There's no way you were ever a Boy Scout, but I'm going to hold you to your promise anyway."

Josh surveyed the room. As far as indoor romantic picnics went, he'd nailed it. And it was only the beginning of what he had planned for them this weekend. Tomorrow he wanted them to leave early for his home in Bar Harbor. Of all the properties he owned, it was the one he considered not only his home but also his private retreat. Situated on almost eleven acres of land, the house overlooked Frenchman Bay and was a short drive to both Arcadia National Park, a place he'd spent countless hours hiking, and the Regency Marina, where he kept his sailboat moored.

In the years he'd owned the home, only his daughter and Evan had been there. And he'd never invited anyone else except his dad and sister, neither of whom had ever felt like making the drive. He wanted to take Courtney there and include her in a part of his life he didn't open to anyone else.

Two months ago, he wouldn't have imagined he'd be planning to bring a woman to his house in Maine. Since he'd moved in with her, the connection he'd sensed in Hawaii had grown stronger. During the day, she frequently popped into his thoughts. He loved making her smile, talking about whatever popped into their heads, and pleasuring her to the point she called out his name.

Back in December when he sat down at her table, he'd wanted nothing but some fun with a beautiful woman. And a few weeks ago, he'd proposed the marriage charade so he'd get back joint custody of his daughter, not because he wanted someone to spend his life with. But he no longer wanted Courtney as a means of winning a custody battle or as a sexual partner to pass the time with. He wanted her and everything a real relationship entailed. Given their history, it might take some work on his part to convince her he was no longer acting when it came to them.

The picnic tonight and their getaway to Maine were his first steps to achieving his goal.

"What happened in here?" Courtney asked, stopping in the doorway. She'd changed into flannel pajama bottoms and a snug-fitting, rose-colored top that didn't quite reach her navel.

She'd left the top two buttons of the top undone, and his fingers itched to slip the next two free so he could spread the shirt open and get a good look at the breasts he fully intended to taste later tonight.

"We talked about going on a picnic in Hawaii but didn't get to it. Since it's too cold outside, I brought it inside."

To give him more room on the floor, he'd pushed aside much of the furniture. Then he'd covered the floor with a blanket he picked up at the mall. While there, he'd purchased both real candles and battery-operated ones, because starting a fire tonight wasn't on the agenda. The real ones were placed on the various tables in the room, while he'd set the battery ones on top of the blanket along with the plates and flowers.

"Candles at a picnic?" She moved closer to him, and the scent he now knew came from the jasmine shampoo and body-wash she kept in the shower teased him.

"First for everything." He poured them each a glass of sparkling white wine and handed her one.

Taking a sip, she knelt down on the blanket-covered floor. "Looks like we have a little of everything."

He'd entered Press, a trendy café on Benefit Street, unsure of what he wanted. Unfortunately, all the menu items sounded good. He'd walked out with everything from roasted broccoli artichoke dip and prosciutto melon skewers to mini cheese-burger flatbread pizzas and roasted cherry tomatoes with fresh mozzarella as well as a handful of other dishes. Before returning home, he'd stopped in Ambrosia and picked up some dessert. A picnic wasn't complete without some sugary treats.

"Yeah, I should never order food when I'm hungry." Which he still was. He'd been close to digging into the pizza when his dad called. "My dad and Laura came back early from their vacation. They wanted to get together this weekend." Josh added as much food to his plate as he could.

After putting a spoonful of dip on her plate, she added

several carrots and celery sticks. Carrots he'd eat raw or cooked. Celery, though, he avoided. Not only did he dislike the taste, it never filled him up and usually ended up getting stuck between his teeth.

"We can go if you want. You met my family."

"Not this weekend. I want to take you up to Bar Harbor in the morning or when you get done with work. We can come back Sunday night. Or if you can work from home for a few days, we can stay longer."

"Uh... yeah, I can work from home tomorrow and on Monday. But I have a meeting on Wednesday morning, so we'll need to be back by Tuesday night." Her eyes reflected the various questions or maybe they were doubts going through her head. Josh wasn't sure.

"If there's something else you want to do, name it."

The questions remained in her eyes as she shook her head. "A weekend in Maine sounds nice."

He heard the *but* in her voice. "Whatever you're thinking, spit it out. You won't offend or upset me."

She chewed on her bottom lip and added an assortment of foods to her plate. Since her eyes never left his face, Josh doubted she knew what she'd even selected. After putting a spoonful of roasted tomatoes practically on top of a slice of pizza, she answered him. "Everyone is buying our story, Josh. We don't need to make it look like we're going on some romantic getaway."

Her words stung. But he should've expected them. "This weekend isn't about anyone else. It's about you and me enjoying some time away from the city in one of my favorite places."

He let his words sink in and dug into his pizza.

Josh was about to try the prosciutto melon skewer on his plate when she spoke again. "What time do you want to leave in the morning?"

"Traffic shouldn't be too bad, but it'd be great if we can get on the road by eight."

Courtney finished the wine in her glass and reached for the bottle. "Shouldn't be a problem as long as Aimee Trainor isn't camped out downstairs again hoping to do an interview with us together."

He'd apologized already, but he felt the need to do so again. "Yeah, I'm sorry I didn't give you a heads-up. How bad was it?" He'd dealt with Aimee so many times he knew how to steer her away from topics he didn't want to discuss. As far as he knew, this was the first time Courtney had dealt with the woman.

She sighed. "It could've been worse, I guess. She probably asked me some of the same questions she asked you, like how we met and kept our relationship a secret."

"Yeah, I got those too." They'd been the first questions Aimee shot off after she cornered him. Then she'd asked how he felt about joining one of the most well-known families in the country. What other questions had she thrown at Courtney?

"She made sure to bring up your reputation and asked how I felt about it," Courtney explained, picking up her fork and spearing a tomato.

Big surprise. If anyone knew about his reputation, it was Aimee Trainor, especially since she'd helped create it. He could check the *Star Insider* website or watch Aimee's show in a few days and possibly learn Courtney's response. But he wanted to know now.

"What did you tell her?"

"I lied." She shrugged and closed her lips around her fork. Once she finished chewing, she sipped her wine and then continued. "I told her I'd seen people change when they fall in love and used Trent as an example. I finished by telling her I knew you loved me. She bought the whole thing."

It might have been a lie at one time. Not anymore. What about for her?

No matter the dollar amount he and Evan had promised to donate, Josh didn't believe she would've agreed to help if she didn't care for him on a personal level. His belief was first backed up when they'd returned from the night at her parents' and she'd asked him to move into her room. Courtney's day-to-day behavior since then reinforced it. If she wanted, she could ignore him. The penthouse was large enough that they could each do their own thing and not bother each other unless they wanted sex. But that wasn't what they did. Instead, they hung out watching television, playing cards, or sometimes chess. Even on the few occasions he'd put on the basketball game, she'd sat in the room with him and read. They never lacked for conversation. And the previous weekend, she'd treated his daughter like she was her own instead of a temporary step-daughter who would pass through her life.

So yeah, he believed she cared about him. But caring about him and loving him was not the same.

"Can I ask you something?" Courtney asked, intruding on his thoughts. "Actually, a couple of things?"

"Shoot."

"Aimee said Naomi called it quits because you cheated on her. Did you?"

He had no proof, but he suspected Aimee had started those rumors to get her ratings up around the same time Naomi ended their relationship.

"If you did, I won't back out of our agreement. I'm just curious."

She made it sound like it didn't matter, but it did. He needed her to believe him. To know he wouldn't cheat on her. "No. Naomi liked the perks of being with me, but she got fed up with the media attention. I've done some stupid things, but the only things I've cheated on were tests in high school." If it hadn't been for Sonya Allen, who sat in front of him freshman year, he would've failed the quizzes his history teacher gave every Friday.

"When she told me, it didn't seem right. It sounds silly, but you don't seem like the cheating type."

Josh raked a hand through his hair. If her other questions stemmed from her conversation downstairs, there was no telling what they might be. "What else did you want to ask?" The more he set straight now the better.

"Yeah, it doesn't matter."

Oh, no way she was getting away with that. She'd piqued his interest, and he wanted to know what was on her mind.

Courtney reached for her glass, but he got to it first and pulled it away. "Come on. Out with it." He held the glass just out of her reach.

Crossing her arms, she stared at him. "You do know I can go in the kitchen and get another glass."

She had him there. Josh handed the glass over. "There are other things I can withhold tonight." He skimmed his hand across her breast on his way to the buttons. "You wouldn't have brought it up if it didn't matter. So ask." He slipped the next button on the shirt free. "I don't want there to be secrets between us."

Her hand closed around his wrist before he moved on to the next button. "If Aimee's right, it's not a secret."

The television host needed to be gagged. "What did she say?"

A hint of pink spread across her cheeks, and she cleared her throat. "That you're rumored to have had threesomes."

"Has never happened. I prefer to dedicate all my attention to one woman." He'd heard the rumor too but never cared enough to find out who started it or to try to stop it. Josh lowered his head toward hers and used his free hand to undo the last button. "Anything else you want to ask?"

"Can't think of anything."

Spreading her shirt open, he cupped her breasts and flicked his thumbs across the already taut nipples taunting him. "I meant what I said about secrets." Josh touched his lips to hers but didn't linger. "If you ever have a question, ask."

He claimed her lips before she could agree or disagree.

THIRTEEN

After closing the garage door, Josh turned off the engine and turned toward the sleeping woman in the passenger seat. After about four hours on the road, they'd stopped to get gas, use the restrooms, and grab some coffee. Less than fifteen minutes after getting back on the highway, Courtney fell asleep, and she hadn't made a peep since. If not for the extra-large coffee, he might have fallen asleep too.

"We're here." He gently shook Courtney's shoulder. Instead of opening her eyes, she mumbled and turned her face toward him. He could carry her inside and then come back for their bags, but unless he had no other choice, he'd rather not. Although Dan, the caretaker who lived in the carriage house with his wife, had cleared the snow from the driveway and probably treated any ice spots, Josh didn't want to risk slipping on black ice on his way to the door while carrying her.

Josh unbuckled his seat belt and nudged her shoulder again. "Courtney, time to wake up. We're here."

She blinked a few times and rubbed a hand down her face before focusing on him. "How long have I been asleep?"

"About an hour and a half."

"Sorry." Adjusting her position, she released her seat belt. "I tried to stay awake. My eyes had other ideas."

"Hey, for the last forty minutes or so, I've been fantasizing about a nap myself." Josh reached into the back seat and grabbed his jacket. Inside the car, it hadn't been necessary, but according to the car's thermometer, the temps outside were hovering in the low teens. Even the short walk from the garage to the house would be unpleasant without a jacket. "You might want to put your hat on." While she'd left her jacket on for the ride, she'd removed her hat following their brief stop at the gas station.

He didn't wait to see if she took his suggestion. Instead, he exited the vehicle and popped the trunk.

"I can take my bag." Courtney met him at the back of the car.

They'd both packed light. "Don't worry about it." After grabbing both bags in one hand, he closed the trunk.

Cold air hit them head-on when they stepped outside, and once again Josh wished the garage was attached to the house. Despite the chilly temperatures, Josh paused and enjoyed the absolute silence around them. Compared to New York or Los Angeles, Providence was a quiet city. However, even in Providence some type of noise was always around. Here, silence prevailed. And rather than tall office and apartment buildings and paved streets, various trees surrounded the property, providing them with ample solitude.

"There are a bunch of trails through the woods. If you're up for it, we can take a walk later." There was also a rocky, winding path that went down to the water, but while much of the snow from the last storm had melted and the path should be fairly clear, he didn't want to risk either of them slipping on any ice on the way down.

Releasing his hand, Courtney pulled her hat down lower and then stuck her hands in her coat pockets.

"I'll need my gloves first." She walked alongside him across the driveway and under the large portico. Frequently, he parked under it when it rained rather than drive into the garage.

Josh unlocked the door and followed Courtney inside. Less formal than his father's and especially the Belmonts' homes, the front door didn't open into a grand foyer with hallways leading in different directions or into rooms designed to impress rather than to use. Instead, the small entranceway led into a three-story cathedral living room. Windows and glass doors dominated the outermost wall, providing breathtaking views of Frenchman Bay as well as the hundred-and-thirty-foot granite and bluestone terrace with its outdoor kitchen—a kitchen he could honestly say he'd never used. A granite fireplace took up much of another wall. Hardwood floors matching the beams visible throughout the home filled every room on the first floor except the eat-in-kitchen. And if he didn't want to enjoy a meal in there, he could eat in what was one of Adalynn's favorite rooms, the breakfast nook. Since it made up the first floor of the home's turret, it was circular, and no matter where you sat you had a great view thanks to all the windows. No matter the meal, his daughter insisted on eating in there because it reminded her of a castle from one of her favorite stories.

Courtney looked around the room and removed her jacket. "This isn't what I expected."

He'd spent over a year looking at homes in the area before the listing for this one came up. It'd been described as having a timber frame design. At the time, he hadn't known what that was, but it had sounded about as different from his house in California as you could get. After one look at the pictures on the real estate website, he'd known the property was just what he'd been looking for.

"What were you expecting?" he asked.

Josh left the bags and his jacket near the sofa. Later he'd bring all of it upstairs, but first, he'd start a fire in the fireplace. The previous afternoon he'd called Dan and Tia to let them know he'd be up this weekend so they could get the place ready, which meant there was plenty of firewood on hand and food in the refrigerator. Somewhere in their late forties or early fifties, the couple had worked for the Monahans, the previous owners of the home. When Josh purchased the property, the Monahans had given Dan and Tia a glowing recommendation and suggested he consider keeping them on. He'd taken their advice and hadn't regretted his decision once. While Dan took care of maintenance both inside and outside and supervised any contractors hired, Tia took care of the general cleaning and food shopping when Josh stayed at the home.

"Something more like... I don't know exactly." She shrugged and moved closer to one of the glass doors leading outside. "Maybe Sara and Christopher's place."

He'd never seen her cousin's home. Josh did know Sara and her husband lived in Alicante, a small, wealthy town located about an hour from Sacramento. Considering where it was located, he had a fairly good guess of what she'd been expecting. Actually, the house he owned in Malibu probably would've met her expectations. Personally, he much preferred this place. Nowhere other than here did he feel at home.

Well, maybe that wasn't 100 percent accurate anymore. Each day that passed, Courtney's penthouse felt more and more like home. Still, all the other properties he owned felt more like vacation spots, places he stayed when he needed a place to sleep. None were places he wanted to spend any length of time at.

He paused in arranging the firewood and stood. "You don't like it?"

Evan disliked the place and told him so every time he came to visit. He insisted the property's only redeeming quality was the view. Josh didn't care what his brother thought. The guy didn't have to live here. Courtney didn't have to live here either, and it was possible this would be her only visit. Regardless, her opinion mattered to him. He wanted her to enjoy visiting and feel as relaxed as he did whenever he walked inside.

"That's not what I said." She turned away from the windows and joined him by the fireplace. "I love it. It's different from what I'm used to. I'm glad we came up this weekend." Courtney reached for his hand. "How about we go for a walk before you start the fire?" She led them over to where they'd left their jackets and handed him his first. "You do know how to get one going, right?" Courtney had one arm in her jacket when she asked the question. "Because we'll need it to warm up when we come back inside."

He could think of a great way to warm them up, no fire needed. "Don't worry."

WHILE COURTNEY'S hands and feet remained comfortable, her face was another story. By the time they returned from their walk, Courtney feared she'd never have any feeling in it again. If they spent any significant amount of time outside again on this trip, she'd ask if Josh had a ski mask hanging around she could borrow.

Right now, thanks to the fire and a mug of hot chocolate topped with whipped cream, the cold was a distant memory. Courtney sipped her drink and watched the flames dance. She didn't know why, but she found it oddly hypnotic. Somewhat mesmerized by the fire, it took a moment for her brain to register that the *1812 Overture* was coming from her purse. With Josh upstairs getting his chess set, she had no good reason not to answer the phone—except for the fact she didn't want to be bothered. With their wedding day closing in, she couldn't afford to miss a call pertaining to it.

Courtney took her time getting to her feet and retrieving her purse from the other side of the sofa. By the time she pulled out her phone, it had stopped ringing, but the words *missed call* along with *Mom* remained on the screen. Her mom hadn't said anything else about pushing back the wedding since the night she'd brought Josh by to meet the family. Instead, she'd helped with any task Courtney passed along, not that she'd handed over many responsibilities.

After hitting redial, Courtney resumed her spot near the fireplace. The way she saw it, there was no reason she couldn't talk to her mom and be toasty warm. Marilyn answered immediately.

"Have you been following the weather forecast?" Marilyn asked once greetings were out of the way.

Sometimes she'd check the weather app on her phone when she was trying to decide how to dress or if she was traveling somewhere, but she didn't do so on a daily basis. And she never switched on any of the various weather channels. As far as she was concerned, she could look outside and see that it was raining or sunny. She didn't need a meteorologist to tell her a day in advance that it might rain, especially when there was nothing she could do to change it anyway.

"No. Why, are we getting snow this weekend?" As long as she was back in Providence in time for her meeting on Wednesday, she didn't care what kind of weather they got over the next day or two.

"Not this weekend," Marilyn replied. "But a severe winter storm with blizzard-like conditions might hit our area next Saturday or Sunday."

When she looked at her phone's weather app yesterday morning, she'd noticed the snowflake icon beside next Saturday. Honestly, she'd dismissed it. She'd never studied meteorology, but she knew the farther out they tried to predict the weather, the less accurate they were. While today they might be telling the public to expect several feet of snow next weekend, in another three or four days they might be saying to expect heavy rain.

"That's a week away, Mom. It might turn into some rain or nothing at all."

"It's possible, but I think you should keep a close eye on the forecast. Maybe even consider pushing the wedding back a week."

Courtney couldn't argue with her mom about following the forecast. She'd rather not postpone the wedding, because if they did it'd be for at least three weeks, which Josh wouldn't like. She knew for a fact Scott and Paige wouldn't be able to come if they pushed it back one week. They were visiting Paige's brother in Virginia the weekend after her wedding. Even if she told him not to change his plans, he'd insist on doing it so he could be there. And the weekend of Valentine's Day was out because her cousin Leah was getting married then. No way did she want to take the spotlight off her cousin's special day. At the same time, she didn't want her family and friends to get stranded in Newport either.

"I'll talk to Josh."

Her mom sighed. "For what it's worth, your dad agrees it would be wise to postpone."

No big surprise there. Her parents tended to agree on most things. It got annoying sometimes.

"And even if the storm isn't as bad as they're predicting here, it's possible not everyone will make it depending on how the weather is in their area. They're saying it's going to affect much of the East Coast," Mom continued, intent on convincing Courtney to take her advice.

"Mom, I'm not making any decision this minute. But I'll

follow the forecast, I promise. When we decide, you'll be the first to know."

This time her mom didn't argue. And after another minute or two of conversation, Courtney ended the call and pulled up her internet browser so she could find a detailed weather report. Sure enough, the meteorologist for one of the Providence-based news stations was predicting that a possible nor'easter would hit the area next weekend, bringing with it several feet of snow. But even he stated it was too early to know for certain if and when the storm would hit. Still, she couldn't dismiss the possibility either.

Josh set the marble chessboard on the coffee table and opened the box containing the black and green pieces that matched the board. "Black or green?" he asked as he started to remove the pieces.

"Doesn't matter."

He moved the green pieces closer to her and then started to place the black ones on the board.

"You look annoyed." Courtney started on her row of pawns.

Finished with the back row, he placed his first pawn on the board. "A little. I planned to wake us up early and take you to Cadillac Mountain tomorrow to watch the sunrise."

With her pawns all on the board, she added the two knights and then reached for the bishops. "I'm guessing it's nearby."

"It's one of the mountains in Arcadia National Park. But I checked while I was upstairs, and the road to the top is closed for the winter. It won't open again until mid-April."

"Makes sense. It's easier to close it than clear the snow all winter." After running through a few different opening moves in her head, she moved a pawn. "We can get up early and watch the sunrise here."

"Between October and March, the mountain is the first

place in the US to see the sunrise. I drove up after I first moved here to see it. There is something different about watching it there." Unlike her, Josh moved his knight first. "We'll have to go in the fall before they close the road."

Not knowing exactly when the custody issue would be settled, they hadn't set an exact end date for their marriage. Instead, they'd agreed to make a decision once the court did. But October was eight months away, and a lot could happen in eight months.

Josh reached for his hot chocolate and waited for her to make another move. "Have you ever visited the park?"

Shaking her head, she concentrated on the various chess strategies she knew. When it came to the game, she wasn't an expert but could usually hold her own against most opponents. "This is the first time I've been up here."

"When it's nicer, we'll have to do some hiking."

The only hiking she'd ever done had been with Josh in Hawaii. The trail they took had been long but relatively flat. She expected anything they tried here wouldn't be the same. "I've never done any real hiking."

"There are some basic trails that even Adalynn can handle. We can start with those and work up to the more challenging ones."

"We'll definitely need a trail equivalent to a bunny slope." If his four-year-old daughter could handle hiking, she better be able to as well. "While you were upstairs, my mom called. Next weekend we might be getting a nor'easter. She thinks we should postpone the wedding." Courtney moved her next piece and leaned back against the sofa. "I checked the weather forecast. If the storm hits, we could get several feet of snow. But right now it's still an if."

"Damn it." Josh raked a hand through his hair and frowned. "What do you want to do?"

"It's a week away. Half the time they don't get the weather

for tomorrow right, so we might be worrying about nothing. And rescheduling everyone might be hard." If the band and photographer she'd hired couldn't accommodate whatever new date they selected, she'd have to find new ones. She didn't relish the idea. "But if we do get the storm, it'll make travel tough. Maybe impossible for some."

The frown lines on his forehead deepened. "Would we just push it back a week?"

She shook her head. "It'd have to be more like three. Scott has plans the following weekend. I don't want him to cancel them for this. And we're not getting married the same weekend as Leah."

The game forgotten, Josh leaned forward and rested his elbows on his knees. "We could cancel the wedding altogether and have your uncle marry us in his office when we get back to Providence. Problem solved."

Her reply required no thought. "No. It's too late for that route. Mom gave me a hard enough time when I told her we were getting married so soon. If we have Uncle Mark marry us in his office, she'll start again. And she wouldn't be the only one to find it strange if we did that." And Courtney wouldn't blame her. In her mom's shoes, she'd be suspicious too.

"Then what do we do?"

"It's only Friday. Let's wait until Sunday night and see what the forecast says. If it still looks like we going to get the storm, we postpone. And try to reschedule for the weekend after Valentine's Day."

She'd prefer a more definitive solution, but for now, it was the best she had.

FOURTEEN

Josh had planned it all out on the drive up yesterday. He'd grab some muffins or bagels from the kitchen, fill a couple of travel mugs with coffee, and wake Courtney up early. Then they could enjoy breakfast at the top of the mountain and watch the sunrise. It never entered his mind that the road up would be closed this time of year. At least he'd checked before putting his plan into action. And they'd still watched the sun come up this morning while eating cinnamon chip muffins and drinking coffee. They simply did it from the comfort of the living room. As far as mornings went, they didn't get much better. After breakfast, they headed to Arcadia and drove along the two portions of Park Loop Road that remained open all year. The first of the two had taken them along the ocean and by Sand Beach and Thunder Hole, a natural rock inlet that got its name thanks to the thunderous sound produced in the area when the right size wave rolled into it. The second brought them over toward Jordan Pond. From there they'd driven to the downtown area and parked. During vacation season, it was almost impossible to find a place to park. Actually, the local community encouraged visitors to use the Island Explorer shuttle, a free public transportation system that operated during the peak months to get around the area. This time of year, not many people visited, and today he'd had his choice of spots.

Unlike yesterday when the temps lingered in the teens, right now they were in the high thirties. Since the weather seemed to be cooperating, at least today, they were taking advantage of it. And for the past hour or so they'd been exploring the various stores and art galleries.

"A café for dogs." Courtney stopped in front of the store on their right. A sign in the shape of light brown dog biscuit hung over the door with the words Your Best Friend's Café carved into it. Another dog bone was on the glass door with the words Your Best Friend's Cafe: Gourmet Baked Goods and Gifts. In the window, there was a display of cupcakes similar to what you'd see in a regular bakery along with toys and coffee mugs, each one featuring a different dog breed.

Josh moved closer to the window for a better look inside. "It's for dogs with more refined tastes." Although not crowded, guests sat at several of the café's tables while their furry best friends lounged on the floor near them. "Do you want to go inside? They have normal bakery stuff too."

"Up to you. I'm not starving, but if you're hungry, we can get something."

Hungry, no. Curious, yes. He loved dogs, but it'd been years since he owned one. He opened the door and held it for her. "You can pick the next stop."

Two long display cases flanked either side of the counter. It didn't take a genius to figure out what case contained the bakery treats for the four-legged customers and which one held those for the customers on two legs, thanks to the labels inside. While the café occupied half the store, anything and everything a dog owner could want for their best friend or themselves filled the other side.

A woman stood in front of them at the counter. A dog dressed in a blue flannel jacket and boots stood by her feet.

"Do you know what you want?" Josh eyed the various beverages listed on the board. After getting a good look at the bakery items available for dogs, he'd half expected to see premium beverages listed for them too. But it looked like the only drink served to dogs was water.

"White chocolate latte and a cinnamon biscotti."

"Human or dog variety?" He couldn't resist, especially since everything in both cases looked tasty. In fact, if someone handed him a cookie or cupcake intended for a dog, he wouldn't have known it just by looking at it.

"Human. But if you want to get yourself a Carob Woof biscuit, I won't let Aimee Trainor or any of your fans know."

"It does look good. I think the golden retriever over there might be eating one." The dog in question was going to town on something. "But the Corgi Cupcake with peanut butter frosting looks good too."

Tray in hand, the customer ahead of them and her four-legged friend walked away, and they moved forward as more customers entered the store and joined the line.

"Get one of each," Courtney suggested with a shrug. "You can take one home with you."

The employee behind the counter didn't look in their direction as she popped something into the microwave. "Be right with you," she said before walking through the door behind the counter.

When the employee returned, she carried a new tray of frosted cookies. Josh couldn't tell whether the cookies were for people or dogs.

"Sorry about...." The woman's voice trailed off as she stared at Josh. Her eyes darted in Courtney's direction before zooming back toward Josh. "Oh. My. God. J.T. Williamson." Keegan, according to her name tag, glanced at Courtney again.

"You were both on the cover of *Today Magazine* this week. I read it every week. I can't believe you're in here." She pulled a cell phone from her back pocket. "No one will believe me without a picture."

A handful of pictures later, Josh set their tray down and pulled out a chair. Right away the dog at the next table, a breed he didn't recognize, came over to say hello.

"Sorry about that. Max likes to make new friends," the dog's owner said.

Josh gave the pooch a scratch behind the ears. "Don't worry about it. What kind of dog is he?" He looked a bit like a pug but not quite.

"A jug." The woman piled her napkin and empty plate back on her tray.

Maybe he needed his hearing checked. Had the woman called her dog a jug?

"A jug?" Courtney asked.

Good, at least she'd heard the same thing as him.

Max's owner smiled and nodded. "Silly name, I know. He's part Jack Russell and part pug." Picking up her tray, she slipped the dog's leash back on her wrist and left.

He watched the dog leave. It'd be the perfect size for Adalynn. She'd been after him since the previous winter for a dog. When she mentioned it during a video call in the fall, he'd promised they would talk about it later. There hadn't been enough time during his two short visits with her since then.

"My last dog was a Jack Russell. Her energy level was through the roof."

Across from him, Courtney removed her gloves and set them aside. "You had a dog? I pictured you as more of a cat person."

There'd been two of those in the house growing up, but they'd been his sister's pets. "Nope. Dog guy. Lizzie died in her sleep five years ago." And he'd been relieved she'd gone on her own. "She was about fourteen." He wasn't positive of her age. When he adopted her from the shelter, they estimated she was already seven. "Adalynn wants a dog. And I miss having one. After the court case and stuff is settled, I might start looking for one."

"Why wait? Look when we get back." She stirred her drink and then lifted the mug, which featured a picture of a Collie on one side and a dog bone with the name of the café on the other. "I like dogs."

"Maybe."

SHE'D LOST HER MIND. What other explanation could there be for her telling Josh to look for a dog when they got back? It wasn't that Courtney hated dogs. Even though she'd only had one in her life, she liked them. But the last thing she wanted was to get attached to a dog, because at some point Josh would move out and take the dog with him. Whether it happened two months from now or in eight months, it would be difficult enough. She saw no need to add to the pain.

And no question about it, there would be a lot of pain—a fact she could only blame on her herself. She'd told herself from the beginning to keep her distance and make sure their relationship stayed platonic. But had she listened to her advice?

Nope.

She'd done the complete opposite and let him into every aspect of her life. Now there was no turning back.

Yep, her heart was fully invested in their charade, whether or not she liked it.

With a sigh, Courtney tore her eyes away from Josh, who was working on a fire, and back toward the chess game they'd started when they returned. He'd won last night's game, and she wanted to beat him tonight.

At the sound, he turned away from the fireplace, a bunch of kindling in his hand. "Something wrong?"

Yeah, I love you. If she told him and he didn't feel the same, it'd make the next several months of living together awkward. Perhaps at some point she'd risk it and tell him the truth but not tonight.

"Just wishing we bought some Schnauzer doodle cookies. They looked good." A little humor was just the thing to lighten her thoughts.

"We can go back tomorrow and grab a Boxer Biscotti too. Or you can order online and have them shipped to you."

"Maybe we should wait until you have a dog to feed them to," she suggested.

Josh went back to arranging the wood while she focused on the chess pieces. If she had any hope of winning, she needed to keep her mind on the game, not Josh's cute ass or the way she felt about him. Her cell phone on the coffee table rang before she settled on her next move.

A glimpse at the screen confirmed the caller. "It's my sister."

Had her mom enlisted Juliette's help in convincing her to postpone the wedding because of the possible storm? Courtney dismissed the notion as quickly as it came. If her mom had enlisted anyone's help, it would be her brother's. Before she picked up the device, Josh's phone rang too.

After checking it, Josh looked back at her. "Be right back. It's Ben."

She didn't know who Ben was, but with Josh gone for the moment, she'd see what her sister wanted.

"Welcome to the club." Juliette skipped a proper hello.

"Most people start a conversation by saying hi. Some even

ask how the other person is doing," Courtney replied. "What club are you welcoming me to?"

"The being interviewed by Aimee Trainor one. Your little heart-to-heart was on the show last night."

Courtney rolled her eyes. That was one club she didn't care to be a part of.

"My favorite part was your response when she brought up Josh's past. Reminding her of how similar Trent had been before meeting Addie was brilliant. It really drove your point home."

She was glad Juliette approved. At the time she hadn't considered how Trent might feel about having his past brought up. If she could redo the interview, she would've left his name out of it. "Since when do you watch her show?"

"Usually I don't, but Tory called and let me know about it. She saw it while at the airport. I couldn't resist checking it out on the website."

On the positive side, Courtney doubted Trent had seen it. Her cousin detested anything and everything about the *Star Insider*. His wife never watched it either, so unless someone told him, he'd never know she mentioned him Thursday night.

"What are you up to tonight?" Juliette asked, thankfully moving away from the interview. "Allison arrived this morning, and Leah's in Providence. I thought we could have a girls' night out since you don't want a bachelorette party. The four of us can spend the night in Boston. Check out the Excalibur."

She loved her sister, but their ideas of a fun night out were vastly different. Even if Courtney was around, she might have come up with an excuse to avoid going out with Juliette and their cousins, because dance clubs weren't her favorite places. She visited them occasionally with her sister or her friends. Often she was ready to leave after about an hour or so.

"Josh and I are up in Bar Harbor until Tuesday."

"Oh. As in Bar Harbor, Maine? What are you doing up there?"

Unless it involved a tropical beach location, her sister preferred to be in and around the city. While Bar Harbor might have a downtown area, it wasn't anything like downtown Boston or New York.

"Josh has a house up here."

"Really? That seems like an unusual spot for him to own a home. Anyway, then I won't see you until the wedding. I'm heading back to New York on Tuesday for a few days to take care of some things. I'll be back sometime on Friday afternoon. The wedding is still on, right? Mom's all worried about the storm we might be getting. When I saw her yesterday, she said she would talk to you about postponing."

"She called. And Josh and I decided to wait until Sunday night and see what the forecast looks like." Courtney watched Josh enter the room. Before his cell phone rang, he'd been smiling. He wasn't smiling anymore, but he wasn't frowning either. He simply looked deep in thought.

"Either way, I'll call you." Or maybe she'd send out a group text message to the entire family, letting them know whether or not the wedding was on. She'd worry about it once they decided. "Have a safe drive back to New York." After ending the call, she turned the ringer off on her phone. If anyone called, they could leave her a message.

"Was Juliette calling to tell you about the weather too?" Josh asked as he finished arranging the wood and lit a match, then sat down on the other side of the coffee table.

Courtney shook her head, even though Josh's attention was focused on the flames and not her. "She wanted to share her thoughts on my interview. *The Star Insider* aired it today."

Clearly, something other than their chess game or next weekend's weather was on his mind. She watched his face and waited. When several seconds passed and he remained silent, she spoke up. "Who's Ben?"

Josh exhaled and looked at her. "He's my agent."

"What did he want?"

"To talk about a role. The studio is doing a sequel to *Over The Edge*. I already told Ben and the producers I'm not interested in doing it. This is the second time he's tried to change my mind. He's not happy I'm not taking on a new project for a while."

His answer didn't jive with his apparent mood change. "Was that all he wanted?"

"Yeah." Standing, he walked toward the fireplace. "But while I was on the phone, I got a text message from Naomi. She wants to meet on Monday."

Yep, that explained the change in Josh's mood. "What did you tell her?"

Raking a hand across his face, he walked back to where he'd been sitting. "Nothing yet. My first instinct was to ask when and where. I even started to type that back. But I decided to wait and see what my lawyer thinks first. After I talk to David, I'll answer her."

"She just asked to see you. She didn't mention why?" If she were in Naomi's position, she would've provided a reason for such a meeting.

"Nope. She didn't mention the custody agreement or our lawyers. She only asked to see me."

Talk about frustrating. And if Josh replied asking why, his ex-girlfriend would know he'd read the message, meaning she'd expect an answer to her request before Josh spoke his lawyer. "Do you think David will get back to you soon?"

It was a Saturday, and people had lives. For all she knew, David might have children and spend his weekends coaching their basketball teams or attending gymnastic competitions.

"Don't know. On the weekends sometimes he responds

right away and other times it takes hours. He's got three sons and coaches their hockey teams." Josh retook his seat across from her. "Either way, I'll probably hear from him sometime today."

For Josh's sake, she hoped his lawyer called him sooner rather than later.

"Assuming he doesn't tell me it's a bad idea, I'll meet with her."

She understood why the lawyer might advise against it or perhaps suggest Josh only meet with her if both their lawyers were present. "And if he recommends you don't see her, what are you going to tell her?" He couldn't ignore the text message indefinitely.

"Not sure exactly," he admitted, shaking his head. "But we should probably plan to leave tomorrow instead of Tuesday. I'm sorry."

"We can come back here some other time. Maybe Adalynn can come with us." Much like at his condo in Boston, one of the bedrooms here was clearly intended for his daughter. Located across the hall from the master suite, the room was painted lilac and contained a toy store's worth of stuffed animals and a large barn complete with plastic horses.

"Yeah. I know," Josh replied.

Whether they could come back didn't change the fact that Josh would rather stay here and enjoy having Courtney all to himself. But if Naomi wanted a meeting, he couldn't ignore the request. Too much was at risk. Her decision to seek sole custody had happened with no warning. It was anyone's guess why she wanted to see him. She couldn't make any changes to the temporary custody agreement in place without going before a judge, so that was out. He'd invited her and Adalynn to the wedding because he wanted his daughter there—not that he expected them to come. Naomi wouldn't need to see him to tell him they wouldn't be there.

"Check." Courtney moved her bishop into place.

He should have seen that coming. If he'd been paying closer attention, he would have. But since he'd read Naomi's text, he couldn't think about much else. "You got lucky." Josh moved his king out of danger. Even though he hadn't heard his phone, Josh pulled the device from his pocket and checked for a text message from David.

Nothing. Still. *What the hell is taking you so long?* If his lawyer didn't respond soon, he'd call him again.

"Are there updates on next weekend's weather?" she asked.

He switched over to the weather app and opened the link for the extended forecast. "Hasn't changed."

"Figures." Courtney's hand went toward her knight, but then she pulled it back. "Maybe—"

The ding alerting him to a new message cut off the rest of her statement. "David says meeting with Naomi is up to me. He doesn't see any harm in it." He pulled up the text from Naomi prepared to ask when and where Monday. Like earlier, he paused. "What do you think?" Not only did he value her opinion but, unlike him in this situation, she could make a decision without her emotions getting involved.

She looked up long enough to answer him. "Go see her."

Josh hit Send.

Courtney propped her chin on her left hand while she studied the board, drawing his attention to the ruby masquerading as an engagement ring on her finger. Not that he expected it to happen, but if a miracle occurred on Monday and Naomi announced she'd changed her mind, how would Courtney want to proceed? She'd agreed to help him so he could get joint custody back. If they settled the matter, he no longer needed her help. She might call off the wedding. He'd seen plenty of acquaintances do it. He'd even seen some go back and forth from being engaged to not being engaged. Mark Walden, an actor he'd worked with on two films, and Selena Cruise had broken off their engagement twice before finally getting married. Three months later, they filed for divorce. Both times Mark and Selena called it quits, the media had a field day speculating on the reasons. He'd rather avoid that if possible for several reasons. But Courtney might be willing to tolerate the attention to avoid having to file for a divorce later.

Or maybe not? She valued her family's opinion. What would they think if she canceled less than a week before the wedding?

It doesn't matter. Whatever did or didn't happen on Monday, he intended to do everything he could to keep Courtney in his life permanently.

FIFTEEN

Courtney had checked the weather more times since her mom's call on Friday night than she normally did in a month. Each time she did, she hoped for an update stating the nor'easter would only bring heavy rains or it wouldn't hit them at all. After all the rushed planning, she had no desire to reschedule everything. As of this morning, it appeared the weather gods didn't care about what she wanted. Fingers crossed that something had changed since then.

During the drive back from Maine, she'd refrained from using her phone to log on to the internet. Reading in a moving car usually made her nauseous. She couldn't use that as an excuse any longer. So while Josh brought their overnight bags to the bedroom, she removed her laptop from her briefcase.

After powering on the device, she brought up the website for Channel 10 news. She didn't have to click on the menu link in the top right-hand corner to bring up the forecast. It remained the top story on the channel's homepage. "Okay, meteorologist Belinda Fredericks, give me some good news." She pressed the play button on the screen.

Unfortunately, she got the opposite. The meteorologist

predicted the storm would arrive late Friday night and continue throughout the day Saturday. At the moment, the storm team at the news channel expected winds up to or greater than 35 mph and anywhere from two to three feet of snow. Before ending her report, Belinda recommended everyone make sure they were prepared for the weekend storm and the likely power outages it would cause throughout the area.

With a groan, Courtney rubbed her temples as a mental list of everything she needed to change, rather than a list of things they might want to stock up on from the store, formed. No doubt about it, tomorrow would be a busy day.

"What's the latest?" Josh entered the kitchen and went straight to the refrigerator.

"Not good." She accepted the bottle of cranberry lime seltzer water and twisted off the cap. "Lots of snow and blizzard-like conditions all starting late Friday night. I don't think we really have a choice. Postponing makes the most sense."

She sipped her drink. She'd call her parents first, followed by Scott and Paige. Then she would try calling her uncles, starting with Uncle Mark since he was conducting the ceremony. After that, she'd send a group text message to the rest of her family and the handful of friends she'd invited. Tomorrow, she'd contact the chef at Cliff House, followed by everyone from the florist to the band. Talk about a major pain in the butt.

Josh lowered the bottle from his lips as he sat down next to her. "Must be the day for bad news. My mom called while I was in the other room. She's already in town. Arrived earlier this afternoon."

They'd discussed his mom only once. He'd admitted that the word diva was one way to describe her. Since he'd shared that he didn't want his mom at the wedding, Courtney assumed they didn't have a close relationship and never mentioned her. Instead, she inquired about his dad and younger sister, neither of whom she'd met.

"She wanted to come by tonight and meet you. I told her we have plans with your cousin," Josh explained while he peeled the label off his bottle. "I'm not up for a visit with her tonight. She insisted on tomorrow instead, even suggested you invite your parents to join us." He crumbled the label into a ball and raised the bottle toward his mouth. "If you want, I can give her another excuse when I call to tell her the wedding won't be happening this weekend. I'm fine with that."

She'd met plenty of divas. One more wouldn't make a difference. "Nah. Let her come." Courtney picked up her cell. "I'll call Mom now and let her know about the weekend. I'll invite her and Dad to come over tomorrow."

JOSH PUT his hand over Courtney's before she pulled up her mom's contact information. "How do you feel about me inviting Evan and Shannon tomorrow?" His sister had arrived in the city yesterday and was staying with Evan. And the more people around, the less attention his mom could send Courtney's way.

"Sure."

While Courtney called her mom, he sent off text messages to his siblings. He'd hoped Courtney would say another time would be better. During their conversation, Josh had toyed with telling his mom they were booked solid all week. But knowing his mom, she'd ignore him and show up at their door anyway. She'd done it numerous times. When she visited, he preferred as much warning as possible so he could get his head in the right place—an impossible feat tonight so he'd lied when she asked about coming over. All day his thoughts had gone back and forth from why Naomi wanted to meet with him to whether the wedding would happen on Saturday. At least he had the answer to the second question. All things considered, postponing the wedding was the logical decision, even if he hated it.

Tapping his fingers against the countertop, he watched as Courtney shared the news with her mom. Her hair hung loose, and she was wearing a dark red sweater. The combination brought him back to the first time he saw her sitting by the pool. That afternoon she'd been wearing a modest crimson bathing suit, and her hair had hung past her bare shoulders. He remembered thinking she reminded him of a sexy librarian. Courtney wasn't the type he usually went after; actually, his usual type had been sitting at the table next to her when she'd caught his full attention. It hadn't strayed once since then either. Even during the short time between their last night together in Hawaii and the afternoon she'd walked into his brother's office, no one else had interested him. Instead, his thoughts had routinely traveled back to her.

She kept her conversation short. "Mom and Dad are busy tomorrow." Rather than put the device down, she took a sip of water as she brought up another contact. "I'm going to call Scott and Juliette to let them know. While I'm at it, I'll call my uncles too. Everyone else can get a text message."

While she did that, he'd watch some television and send some messages himself. "I'll be in the family room."

He got responses to all the messages at the same time. His brother, minus his girlfriend, and his sister would join him for their mom's visit. It didn't surprise him that Gemma wasn't coming. Evan hadn't introduced their mom to his girlfriend yet, and he planned to avoid it for as long as possible. The texts from his dad and aunt were similar to each other. Both had been following the weather and had expected they'd postpone the wedding. They'd said to just let them know when it would be.

Josh scrolled through the various *I Love Lucy* episodes.

They'd finished season one and started on season two sometime last week. Halfway down the list, the title "Vacation From Marriage" caught his attention. He remembered the episode. The characters had agreed to temporarily live as if they were all single again. By the end of the show, both couples had reached the conclusion they were happier married. He'd never pictured himself married. Even when he'd been with Naomi, his longest relationship to date, thoughts of proposing had not surfaced. He'd cared about her, but he'd never had any desire to marry her. And after dating as many women as he had, he'd guessed love wasn't in the cards for him.

Courtney sat down next to him and crossed her legs on the sofa. "My family knows the wedding is off."

Damn, he didn't like the sound of that.

"Tomorrow, I'll call the photographer and stuff. Uncle Mark said any weekend works for him. And I'll need to check with Callie about when we can use Cliff House."

They were watching the episodes in order, so he scrolled down until he reached the next one they hadn't seen. Hitting Play, he tossed the remote on the table. While the opening credits played, he put an arm across her shoulders. "Do you need any help?"

"Nah, everyone is used to working with me. I'll take care of it. You focus on your meeting."

That was easy to do. Since the call Saturday, the meeting never left his thoughts.

"Do you want me to come with you?" she asked, looking in his direction.

A knot of emotion formed in his throat. She had a hundred things on her plate but was willing to add another. All the women in his past put their wants first. Courtney didn't—something he'd learned while they were in Hawaii. And it was one of the things he loved about her.

Lowering his head, he brushed his lips across hers. "No."

He kissed her again, this time lingering there a little longer. "You've got the wedding stuff to deal with and work."

He moved in to kiss her again, but she pulled back. "Are you sure? I have this thing called a cell phone. I can use it to make calls on the drive into Boston. And if we were still in Maine, I'd have to do some work tonight since I wouldn't be in the office tomorrow. Instead of watching television, I can go do it now."

He tucked some hair behind her ear, then skimmed his finger across her jaw. "No work tonight. I want you here with me." Josh took possession of her lips before she could protest.

HANGING UP THE PHONE, Courtney dropped her face in her hands. They should have eloped the day after she agreed to Josh's charade. If she could travel back in time, she'd suggest— nope, she'd insist they elope instead of plan a traditional, if small by Sherbrooke standards, wedding. Mom would've been disappointed, but an elopement would have been so much easier.

She should've known it was going to be a hellish day. All the signs were there this morning. They'd started before she brushed her teeth. While in the shower, she banged her head when she bent to pick up the shampoo she dropped. A headache set in soon after. More focused on answering text messages from relatives regarding the wedding, she burned both her eggs and toast not long after the shower incident. Rather than attempt to make more, she settled on the healthiest-looking cereal in the kitchen. The box claimed it was made with whole grain oats. But since the word frosted was also in the title, she doubted the box's contents were all that good for you. Still, pouring a bowl of cereal took less time than cooking more eggs. And honestly, it had tasted pretty good. It would have been even better with some fresh blueberries on top.

Bad luck struck a third time when the handle of her coffee mug snapped off, sending the coffee all over the floor and her dress. While Josh cleaned up the mess, she changed. Even with his help in the kitchen, she pulled out of the garage later than usual.

After zipping through her emails and a quick meeting with Deena in marketing—wedding or no wedding, she had work to do—she called her cousin. Before she tried to reschedule the photographer or anyone else, she needed to know when she could use Cliff House. Thankfully, Callie assured her it was available anytime between now and late spring. Callie even offered to call Henri and let him know the wedding was off this weekend. She considered taking her up on the offer, since it'd mean she had one less thing to do, but she hadn't.

Her conversation with the longtime chef went similar to all the other ones she'd had so far. He, along with probably the entire state, was following the weather forecast and had been since the weekend, so he'd expected she'd push the wedding back.

With the easy calls out of the way, she'd moved down her list. Now she had a slight pain above her right eyebrow and more unpleasant conversations to go.

At the knock on the door, she lifted her head. *Please don't let it be Mom.*

She'd run into Marilyn this morning. While her mom hadn't come right out and said, "I you told a spring wedding would be better," it'd been implied.

Courtney crossed her fingers. "Come in." Her shoulders slumped when Addie walked in, a bakery box and beverage carrier in hand.

"Figured you're going a little crazy rescheduling every-thing and wouldn't want to leave the office. So I grabbed us something while I was out." She set the items down on the desk and sat in the chair opposite Courtney.

"A little crazy? More like a little insane." She accepted the large paper cup from Ambrosia that Addie handed over to her. "Thanks for thinking of me."

"That bad?"

"The photographer I hired isn't available again until the first Saturday in September. The only reason she could do the wedding this weekend was because someone canceled back in December."

For the sake of convenience, she'd settled on a photographer from the area. Now she didn't care where they were based or the price tag she needed to pay to get them here.

"And forget about the band. They're booked solid until July." Worse case, they skipped hiring a band and went with a DJ. Even if they went that route, she needed to find a DJ and a photographer who were both available in three weeks. Uncovering her drink, Courtney sipped the hot vanilla chai latte.

Across the desk, Addie unzipped her purse and pulled out her phone. "It's not the same, but I know a DJ. His parents and mine have been friends for a long time. I can call and see if he's available for... when are you changing the wedding to?"

"Weekend after Leah's wedding. And I just want music. I don't care if it's a live band or not. Heck, I'm tempted to hook my phone up to some speakers and use it to play music."

While Addie made her call and left her DJ friend a message, Courtney opened the box from Ambrosia. She found two golden brown spinach pies inside. Much like the vanilla chai latte, the pies were something she frequently ordered at the café.

"It might be awhile before Dominic calls me back. He works for a computer company in Jamestown and does the DJ thing on the side."

In a perfect world, she'd have everything lined up by the

end of the day. She lived in the real world though, where the outcome you wanted and the one you got frequently didn't coincide.

"Don't suppose you know any photographers."

"Sorry, no." Addie uncovered her drink, stirred it with a spoon, and took a sip before saying anything else. "My cousin dabbles in photography. It's a hobby for him. He's got a ton of equipment, but he only takes pictures of landscapes. You wouldn't want him taking your wedding photos."

Oh, well, it never hurt to ask.

"Maybe you and Josh should push the wedding back further. It might make things easier for you."

You're telling me. She trusted Addie and considered her a close friend, but sharing the real reason wasn't an option. "We'd rather not."

Addie narrowed her eyes a smidge, and Courtney prepared herself for the question clearly on her friend's mind.

It never came. Instead, she shrugged and removed one of the spinach pies from the box. "Maybe you should skip a traditional ceremony and reception. You and Josh could fly to Vegas next weekend and get married. Or ask Mark to marry you in his office sometime this week. There's no rule saying you must have the whole family there."

"Believe me, I'm starting to think you're right."

Maybe they should book a flight and get married in Vegas. She'd want to be surrounded by her family if this was to be her one and only wedding, but it wasn't. Well, it might not be. It was possible once she and Josh divorced she wouldn't fall in love again—a fact she kept safely locked away.

Addie's cell phone on the table dinged, and Courtney crossed her fingers the text was from Addie's DJ friend. Setting aside her drink, Addie reached for her phone. The expression on her friend's face suggested the text wasn't from Dominic.

"Something wrong?"

"I'm not sure." Addie bit down on her lip before continuing. "What's Josh up to today?"

Her question fell in the odd category. "He went into Boston for a meeting." One she hoped was going well. "Why?"

If possible, Addie's pained expression intensified. "Tracey sent me a link to something she saw on Twitter a few minutes ago."

Shouldn't the nanny have more important things to do than check her social media apps?

"Someone took a picture of Josh and a woman together and posted it." Addie handed over her cell phone. "She thought you should know."

Courtney knew who she'd see even before she accepted the device. The knowledge didn't stop the burning ball of fire from taking shape in her chest as she looked at the picture of Josh and Naomi seated across from each other, his hand on her arm.

"Don't people have better things to do than take pictures and post them on social media?" she asked, giving the device back. "That's Josh's ex-girlfriend, Naomi. They have a daughter together. I knew he was meeting her today."

A picture merely showed a single moment, so she couldn't assume too much from it. But at least it appeared Josh's meeting was a civil one. The memory of Josh's hand on Naomi's arm popped up, and the fireball in her chest expanded.

No, the pictured didn't depict a civil conversation. It showed a compassionate one. *She's engaged to another man.* She'd met Naomi's fiancé the afternoon they picked up Adalynn.

And my relationship with Josh is temporary. She'd reminded herself of that so many times now, she'd lost count.

SIXTEEN

As soon as Josh got home on Sunday, he'd reserved the wine cellar at Emilia, his favorite Italian restaurant in Boston, for his meeting with Naomi. Designed to accommodate up to fifty people, the room was located on the ground floor away from the main dining area and bar upstairs. Non-employees only visited this level if they had an appointment with the restaurant's general manager, whose office was down the hall. Tucked away in here, only the four thousand bottles of wine and Tuscan limestone lining the walls would overhear their conversation this afternoon.

"I'll show your guest down as soon as she arrives," the hostess explained, setting two menus on the table.

Food remained the last thing on his mind.

"Would you like to order a drink while you wait?" she asked.

"Not at the moment."

With a slight nod, the hostess walked away, leaving Josh alone with nothing to do but think and wait—two things he'd done more than enough of since Naomi reached out on Saturday afternoon.

At least Naomi didn't keep him waiting long today. Josh wasn't even done reviewing the first page of the menu when the hostess returned with Naomi by her side. After promising them their server would be along soon, the woman left.

Naomi took her sweet time removing her jacket and pulling out the chair opposite him. Today was the first time they'd been alone since she filed for sole custody. He wanted to demand she explain why she'd done it. Or simply ask if she'd lost her mind. But opening any conversation with a demand never ended well, especially when you had no idea of what was in the other person's head.

"The last time I came here, I was with you. It was right before Adalynn was born," Naomi said, breaking the uncomfortable silence in the room. Meeting his eyes, she opened her menu. "Maybe we should order before we talk."

For now, he'd let her set the tone and pace of their conversation. "Whatever you want." He glanced down, selected the first entrée his eyes landed on, and looked back at the woman across the table. Naomi never left the house looking anything less than perfect. This afternoon, everything from her outfit to her hair and makeup exemplified the time and effort she put into her appearance. And no matter how she felt, she made sure she appeared upbeat. Right now she looked anything but. Even with makeup, he could see the dark circles under her eyes hinting at many sleepless nights.

"Do you want some wine?" The restaurant had wine on hand from all over Italy. He'd yet to order some at Emilia and not enjoy it.

"Believe me, I wish I could have some. But I'm pregnant. But don't skip it because of me."

Had she wanted to see him so she could tell him that? Whether or not she and Reggie had a baby didn't matter to him. For all he cared, they could have ten children.

"Congratulations."

"Thanks."

For someone engaged and expecting a baby, she sounded anything but happy. *Not your problem,* he reminded himself.

Their server joined them, putting a temporary halt to their conversation. At this rate, he'd never know why she'd wanted to see him.

"I didn't thank you for meeting me today," she began the moment they were alone again. "There are a few things I want to explain."

"You couldn't do it on the phone?" Sarcasm clung to his words, but this afternoon he was unable to conceal it.

If his tone bothered her, Naomi didn't let on. "Maybe. But it seemed better to do it in person."

He'd give her that. Some topics needed to be discussed in person. "Okay. What do you need to tell me?" This time he kept his tone sarcasm free—at least it was to his ears.

Rather than answer, Naomi tucked a stray piece of hair behind her ear with her noticeably ring-free left hand. The last time he'd seen her, a large diamond ring had decorated her finger.

Odd. But there could be numerous reasons the engagement ring was absent.

"First, I want to apologize. I know I shocked you by filing for sole custody."

Shocked. Pissed off. He could go on and on.

"It wasn't my idea," she continued. "Even before Adalynn and I moved into Reggie's house, he wanted you out of our lives. Sometime in the fall, he started suggesting it'd be in Adalynn's best interest if I had sole custody."

Josh bit back a laugh. When she had access to his money and connections, his reputation hadn't bothered her.

"A lot of his arguments made sense, especially the one about it being better for Adalynn if she didn't split her time between two houses. Right now, it's not a big deal because she's not in school. But soon she will be. She won't be able to stay with you for a month in Maine and go to school in Massachusetts."

He knew exactly when his daughter started school. He'd assumed they'd cross that bridge when they needed to. "And the ones that didn't?"

"I convinced myself Reggie was right."

He clenched his hands rather than share his current thoughts, many of which involved showing Reggie what he could do with his opinions.

"He became more insistent about it around the time we got engaged. Every chance he got, he'd remind me of your less than glowing reputation and how Adalynn needed a better father figure in her life. And it was his idea to claim you threw drunken parties when Adalynn was in the house. I finally gave in and made an appointment with my lawyer not long before the pictures of you and Courtney Belmont appeared in the media. Actually I think my first appointment with the lawyer was the day the first pictures hit the internet."

"The why doesn't matter at this point."

"I know. I know. Still, I wanted you to know the reason behind my decision. None of it matters anymore. This morning I told my lawyer I no longer want sole custody. He's going to file the necessary documents with the court today. It's possible he already has."

Any minute, he'd wake up. Naomi didn't just tell him she changed her mind. "You're dropping your custody suit?"

She nodded, but with their server approaching the table, she didn't offer up any explanation. And damn it, he wanted one. He deserved one.

Their server placed their salads on the table. "Can I bring you anything else?" she asked.

Whether Naomi required something or not, he didn't care. "We're fine for the moment." He waited until the server exited the room. "Why now?" Did it have anything to do with his upcoming wedding?

"Right after my lawyer filed, I had reservations. But I keep telling myself it was best for Adalynn and for Reggie's and my relationship." A healthy dose of bitterness laced the last few words of her response. "We're no longer engaged. He wanted you out of our lives, but at the same time, he was sleeping with a nurse from his office. Adalynn and I moved out of his house on Wednesday."

Yeah, her current mood made sense. "I'm sorry, Naomi."

Tears pooled in her eyes, and Josh placed his hand on her arm. Despite what she'd done, he hated her relationship ended the way it had.

A tear broke free and slipped down her cheek. Naomi brushed it away before she spoke. "I've spent a lot of time thinking about my decision and decided I was wrong. Your personal life aside, you've been a great dad since the day Adalynn was born, and when you're together, I know you put her first. There is no reason whatsoever for us not to share joint custody of Adalynn."

About time you got your head out of your ass. "Where are you staying now?" he asked instead of offering up the thoughts in his head. He knew she'd sold her townhouse after moving in with Reggie. It took time to find a new apartment or house.

"For the moment, at the Sherbrooke Copley Square. My parents offered me their guest bedroom until I find something, but my job is here. I can't move to Vermont even if it is only temporary."

He'd forgotten her parents had bought an old Victorian in Vermont two summers ago and opened a bed-and-breakfast, a lifelong dream of theirs. "Use my condo in the city." The Sherbrooke Copley Square might be the nicest hotel in Boston, but he didn't want his daughter calling it home for any length of time.

"Are you sure?"

"After lunch, pick up Adalynn and meet me there."

Her face said she wanted to accept the offer, but her mouth said something else. "You're sure Courtney won't mind that your ex-girlfriend is using your condo?"

"No. She'll understand."

Whether she minded or not was the least of his worries. With the custody issue off the table, he no longer needed to get married. Thanks to the weather, they'd already changed the date of the wedding. It'd be easy enough to push it back several months and then at some point call off their engagement entirely, two things he didn't want happening.

COURTNEY SLAMMED her closet door closed with a bit more force than necessary. After spending a good portion of the day searching for a photographer, florist, and either a band or DJ for their wedding and not finding three all available when she wanted them, her frustration level was around a nine. The fact she was waiting for Addie's DJ friend as well as a possible photographer to return calls was the only thing keeping it from a ten. She hoped Josh's day had gone better than hers.

She'd expected him to be here when she got home. His mom and siblings were expected in less than half an hour. Before they arrived, she'd like at least a short recap of his meeting with Naomi. If he didn't get here soon, there wouldn't be time. And she couldn't imagine waiting until their company left to find out what his ex-girlfriend had wanted.

After pulling on a sweater, she added her dress to the dry cleaner bag. Courtney didn't know what Scarlett Basto would be wearing tonight, but she wouldn't look like she'd just left the office. From the little she'd read about the woman, it was more likely Josh's mom would be dressed for a night at a dance club.

Before she left the room, Courtney grabbed her phone and turned off the lights.

Where are you? She typed the message as she walked toward the kitchen.

She'd prefer to have Josh here when his family arrived, especially his mom. She'd met Evan, and from what the brothers had told her, she got the impression Shannon was a lot like them. If there was any truth to Scarlett's reputation, she was nothing like her children. Frequently, the media referred to her as someone others in Hollywood hated to work with because of her ridiculous over-the-top demands.

She got a response almost right away.

Just parked in the garage.

He'd have to give her the extra-condensed version of his meeting, but at least she wouldn't have to welcome his family alone.

"Sorry I'm running so late." Josh walked in carrying several takeout bags. They'd talked about going out for dinner with his family. Josh felt it was a better idea to stay here. Since they both had obligations today, they'd decided to go the takeout route tonight.

"Did you leave Boston later than you planned?" Rush hour traffic out of the city sometimes started as early as three. Depending on when he left, he might have run right into it.

"Yeah. After I saw Naomi, I took care of a few errands. I should've known better."

She glanced at her watch. Unless their guests were late, they didn't have much time. "Give me the abridged version for now. What did she want?"

Josh tossed something he'd pulled from a bag into the refrigerator and turned back toward her. "To explain why she filed for sole custody and to tell me she changed her mind.

We're going back to the way things were before she got the lawyers involved." The happiness radiating off him nearly blinded her.

Joy washed over her, and she threw her arms around him. "That's awesome." As quickly as the joy came, it receded. A combination of dread and curiosity took its place. "What made her change her mind?" They weren't married yet. If just the idea of him getting married was enough, she could have changed her mind weeks ago.

"Finding out her fiancé was screwing a coworker. It's a long story. I'll tell you later."

Dread overshadowed her curiosity. "It had nothing to do with you getting married?" She dropped her arms by her sides and took a step back.

As if connected to a light switch, his happiness went off, and he shook his head. "No. Looks like you're off the hook."

Off the hook. What a way to put it.

"Did you have any luck setting everything up for the weekend after Valentine's Day?" he asked.

"Not yet. I'm waiting for a few people to call me back." This might be the first time a lack of success turned out to be a positive thing.

He shoved his hands in his pockets and blew out a deep breath. "Okay. Then we could push the wedding back several months and then in a month or two call it off altogether."

A fist closed around her throat. She only had herself to blame for being in this position. If she'd kept this a strictly business agreement, her heart wouldn't be tearing in half. "You're not known for your commitment, so nobody would be surprised if it happened." She somehow managed to get the words out.

"Or we could—" The doorbell rang, and Josh closed his eyes. "Damn it."

My sentiments exactly. She wanted to finish this conversation, not entertain his family while still pretending they'd soon be married. "I got it."

He grabbed her arm before she took more than a step. "They can wait a minute." Whoever stood at the door disagreed, because the doorbell chimed again before he continued.

"We've got all night to talk, Josh."

He didn't stop her when she pulled her arm away.

If a bell curve for mothers existed, Scarlett Basto and Marilyn Belmont would be at the opposite tails, something Courtney realized the moment she opened the door. As she expected, Josh's mom wasn't dressed as if she'd recently left the office. For her first meeting with her son's fiancée, the woman opted for white pants, a skintight leopard print body-suit with a plunging neckline, and heeled boots that ended just below the knee. The woman looked like she should be going on stage as a dancer at a concert, not spending a quiet night with her adult children. As if to support Courtney's original opinion, Shannon was wearing jeans and a pink sweater.

Evan arrived moments after his mom and sister, and Courtney quickly learned why Scarlett possessed the reputation she did. After introductions, she spent a solid ten minutes complaining about the cold and informing them they should've planned their wedding for somewhere in California or at the estate she and Trevor owned in Aruba. Her next complaint came when she learned Josh didn't have her favorite wine on hand. Her problem with his choice of dinner quickly followed. Evidently, he was supposed to know she'd become a vegetarian before Christmas. Of all her complaints, the last was one Courtney could do something about. Press, a café in the city, had a full vegetarian menu, and it delivered.

"You're not the type of woman Josh is usually attracted to," Scarlett said.

They'd made it halfway through dinner without another

complaint. Courtney doubted the stretch would last much longer.

"It shocked me when those pictures of you together popped up in December. And I didn't expect him to get engaged. He's too much like me." She smiled in Josh's direction. "Not that there's anything wrong with that. You should have fun when you're young. But I made the mistake of getting married before I should have."

"Mom, you got married when you were twenty-two. Josh is a little older than that. Besides, it's about marrying the right person, not about how old you are when it happens." Shannon spoke up. So far tonight she'd helped move Scarlett off more than one topic when she went off on a tangent.

Scarlett finished her wine and refilled the glass. "Well, there's no doubt your father wasn't the right person for me. Marrying him was the worst decision I ever made. And that's saying a lot."

Courtney couldn't decide if she should laugh or cry. The woman clearly didn't think before she spoke. And Courtney could honestly say she'd never met anyone quite like Josh's mom. If tonight was the one and only time they spent time together, she'd be okay with that. However, there was one benefit to Scarlett's personality. Rather than focus on the conversation she and Josh needed to finish, she put all her energy into trying to predict what the woman would say next.

"But the good thing about marriage, it doesn't have to be permanent," Scarlett added, eliciting something similar to a groan from Josh.

"Have you thought any more about the role in *The Water's Edge*?" Shannon asked.

With that simple question, Josh's mom launched into what Courtney guessed was her favorite subject: Scarlett Basto and her career.

SEVENTEEN

"And Shannon wonders why I haven't introduced Gemma to Mom yet." Seated across from them, Evan propped his ankle on his knee. "The woman never shuts up. I don't know how Trevor lives with her."

Following dinner and perhaps a few glasses of wine too many on Scarlett's part, Josh's sister drove their mom back to her hotel. While Courtney had enjoyed visiting with Shannon and wouldn't mind getting to know her better, she'd been more than happy to see Scarlett leave. The woman had one of those personalities that few people could handle for any length of time. And Courtney wasn't one of those people. She hoped any future interactions with Josh's mom turned out to be much shorter than tonight's visit.

It might be your only interaction. She'd pushed the thought of their pending conversation away during dinner. Now, it was attempting to climb out of the box she'd shoved it in. Until Evan left, she needed it to stay in there.

Josh sat down next to her, but he didn't reach for her hand or put an arm over her shoulders like he usually did. "He travels. A. Lot."

"If I was married to her, I would too," Evan said with a grin very similar to Josh's. It didn't stick around. "Have you heard when the custody hearing will be?"

"There isn't going to be one. Naomi changed her mind. She no longer wants sole custody."

The man's smile returned. "Congrats. You must be relieved. Why didn't you tell me?"

"It happened this afternoon, and I didn't want to discuss it with Mom here."

"Does she even know?" Evan asked.

"No. Half the time, I do not think Mom remembers she has a granddaughter."

Evan laughed sarcastically. "As far as Adalynn is concerned, I'm not sure that's a bad thing. Are you going to go through with the wedding as planned or what?"

Josh glanced at her before answering. "We haven't figured that part out yet. Courtney and I were talking about it when Mom and Shannon got here."

"My advice, make an announcement saying you've decided to wait until the summer. Then in another month or two, have Courtney call off the engagement altogether. She can make up a reason. Maybe one of you wanted kids right away and the other didn't. Something that doesn't reflect poorly on either of you." Advice offered, Evan stood up.

Please say you're leaving. A week ago she wouldn't have cared if Evan stuck around and visited for another two hours.

"Do you have any beer in the kitchen? Or some vodka?" Evan asked instead of saying goodbye. "After a few hours with Mom, I need a drink." At dinner, everyone but Evan, who disliked wine, had at least one glass of it.

"There are a few different kinds in the refrigerator. If you want vodka instead, there's some at the bar," she answered. Although she didn't use it often, the penthouse contained a bar, and she kept it stocked for anyone who visited.

"I'm going to grab something too. Do you want anything?" Josh asked, standing as well.

"All set."

She watched the two brothers walk toward the kitchen. Once they were no longer in sight, she slumped back against the sofa. She liked Evan, and while Josh denied it, the brothers most certainly shared some personality traits. And Evan willingly shared details about Josh's past, such as the fact he'd slept with a bedroom light on until the age of nine because he hated the dark. Regardless of all that, she wished the man would leave so they could get back to the elephant in the room. Or more precisely, the elephant in the room before the doorbell rang and disturbed them.

Alone and with no other distractions, their earlier conversation replayed through her mind. The next words out of Josh's mouth after admitting their upcoming wedding had nothing to do with Naomi's decision has been "looks like you're off the hook." Not long after, he'd offered up a solution almost identical to Evan's suggestion.

The doorbell had cut off Josh's second idea, but she expected it would be something along the same lines. Would he view the situation differently if she told him how she felt? Based on his past relationships, Josh preferred to keep his romantic entanglements short and sweet. That wasn't to say he didn't care about the women he got involved with, but he never fell in love with them. And while she believed he cared about her, from an emotional standpoint, nothing suggested he viewed their relationship much differently than all his past ones.

But if given enough time, could she change that?

You can't make someone love you. A person either fell in love with you or they didn't. So it might be in her best interest to go along with Evan and Josh's suggestion. At the same time, she could ask Josh to move back into a guest room and put an end to their physical relationship.

Sometimes the more time two people spend together, the more likely it will happen. Her conscience sent a counterargument to its first statement.

With a groan, she closed her eyes and wished Josh had never sat down at her table. If he'd joined the women next to her, she might never have met him.

"Too bad Naomi didn't find out about Reggie weeks ago," Evan said after Josh finished filling him in on his conversation with his ex. "At least she told you before the wedding. And the storm gave you the perfect reason to postpone and decide on a way to get out it."

Get out of it? He didn't want to get out of it. If not for the incoming nor'easter, he'd marry Courtney this weekend as planned. Then he'd keep trying to prove he married her because he loved her, not because an agreement existed between them.

"Although I'm not sure you want that," Evan added. "You don't take anyone up to Bar Harbor except Adalynn. Except for me, Dad, and Shannon, you've invited no one to visit you there. But you brought Courtney for the weekend." His brother crossed his arms and leaned against the counter. "You're not acting, bro. This is real for you."

Josh nodded. He saw no point in denying it.

"What are you going to do?" When it came to being nosy, Evan could be worse than an eighty-year-old town gossip.

"I've got an idea. And that means I need your ass out of here." He hated kicking his brother out, but he'd endured enough torture already tonight. Every minute his brother remained only prolonged it.

Pushing off the counter, Evan put his almost empty beer

bottle down. "Shoot me a text later and let me know what you two decide to do."

Courtney remained in the same spot, her head tipped back and her eyes closed, when he walked back into the living room. A night with his mom was an experience. If she needed a few minutes to regroup, he didn't blame her.

"Evan said goodbye." Although he had his choice of places to sit, he retook his spot on the sofa beside her.

Slowing raising her head, she opened her eyes. "He doesn't get along well with your mom."

"They've always butted heads, even when we were kids. Now, he only sees her when he has no other choice. And Mom doesn't come this way often. She prefers the West Coast or her and Trevor's place in Aruba. Tonight's the first time I've seen her in months."

He needed Courtney to know that being with him didn't mean she had to spend a lot of time with his mom. Hell, even he preferred to keep their visits at a minimum, and she was his mother.

"I bet your brother appreciates that."

"You have no idea."

His comment earned him a small smile. But it didn't last long. "Earlier you didn't have time to tell me much about your meeting. What did Naomi's fiancé have to do with her seeking sole custody?"

"I'll tell you later." He'd waited long enough. Before they left this room, they'd finish their earlier conversation. "Right now, we need to make a decision."

"You and Evan had the same idea. And it's not a bad one. People will just think we rushed to get engaged and realized we weren't right for each other. It happens all the time."

Over the past few hours, she'd clearly put some thought into this.

"Before your mom got here, it sounded like you had

another idea," she continued, crossing her legs in front of her on the sofa.

"We could stick to the original plan." *Minus the divorce later down the road.* "If you've got a better idea, I'm listening."

The corners of Courtney's mouth turned downward as she shook her head. "No. Those seem like our only options. And either would work. What do you want to do?"

Her questions caused his stomach to coil up into half a dozen knots. He'd rehearsed this in his head. Unless she automatically insisted they go with his first suggestion, he knew how he'd respond. But just because she hadn't jumped at the chance to never marry him didn't mean he'd like the answer when he offered up his third and final idea.

Spit it out. He swallowed and ran his tongue across his bottom lip. "I want to marry you. Not because people think we're engaged and are expecting it. And not because it'll help me look like a better father." Earlier, he'd removed the engagement ring he bought before leaving Boston from its box and shoved it in his pocket. He reached for it now. "I want to marry you because I love you."

Since they'd been together, he'd noticed many of her rings consisted of rubies. She had several sapphires and emeralds too. This afternoon, he hadn't bothered to look at the diamond engagement rings on display. Instead, he went with a ruby similar to the one she'd been wearing on her left hand all month.

Before she responded, he reached for her hand. There hadn't been time to get the ring sized, so at the moment it was big enough to fit his finger.

"You...." She glanced down at his hand and then at him again. Slowly a smile spread across her face, and she nodded. "You should've started with that suggestion." Leaning closer, she cupped his face and rested her forehead against his. "I love you too."

He'd never known it was possible for an entire body to sigh with relief. But his did. Before he shared the words in his head, he claimed her lips for a single kiss. Later, he'd devote more time to her lips and the rest of her body. Right now he wanted to get out the thoughts in his head while he still could, because once he got her into bed, talking would be at a standstill for a while.

"I don't know what kind of wedding you really want. If you want something more like what your cousins Trent or Gray had, we can postpone for as long as you want."

He'd attended Trent's wedding and seen pictures of Gray's. A lot of planning and money had gone into both. If that was what she wanted, he'd go along with it. The kind of wedding they had didn't matter to him, as long as they were together.

She shook her head with no hesitation. "Tomorrow I'll make some more calls. If I can't arrange everything for a weekend in February, we'll take Jake's suggestion. Then we can plan a party to celebrate in the summer."

He liked her idea. Still, he had to ask. "Are you sure? You might regret it later."

"Positive. The only person I need there is you."

EIGHTEEN

COURTNEY GLANCED AROUND at the guests dancing inside Cliff House's ballroom. Thanks to Addie's DJ friend and a photographer her sister knew in New York, they'd managed to pull everything together in a little over three weeks. They'd also invited a few more guests than originally planned. Except for two people, everyone was here, including Uncle Warren and Aunt Elizabeth, the last two people she'd expected to make it. Not only was Uncle Warren in full campaign mode but also he'd already taken time out of his schedule to attend her cousin's wedding the weekend before.

She glanced across the room to where her mom and dad sat with her mom's three brothers and their wives. Everyone in the family might not always agree, but they let nothing come between them. And no matter what, there was always someone there to help and support you. In her opinion, that characteristic made her family special and unique. She just hadn't realized how unique until she met Josh. His mother hadn't told them whether or not she'd be at the wedding until this past Wednesday, and she hadn't arrived in Rhode Island until late this morning. Honestly, Courtney wasn't disappointed by Scarlett's late arrival or quick departure, since it limited the amount of time she spent with Josh's mom. And while Josh had an aunt and uncle as well as two cousins he was close to and who were all here tonight, he also had an uncle and a cousin he hadn't seen or talked to in over ten years.

"Adalynn is a cutie, but she never stops talking," Juliette said.

Courtney's gaze shifted from her family and toward the dance floor where Josh and his daughter were dancing. Sure enough, Adalynn was talking her dad's ear off.

Not allowing Adalynn to attend the wedding had been another dictate from Naomi's ex-fiancé. During their lunch meeting weeks ago, Naomi promised to bring Adalynn to the wedding. Then starting on Monday, she would stay with them in Providence for two weeks. They'd already had one of the guest bedrooms redecorated for her and filled it with more toys than necessary.

Soon they'd need to redecorate another bedroom—not that Josh knew that yet.

"Pot, meet kettle," her cousin said. Allison and her fiancé, Rock, had traveled up from Virginia for the wedding.

Juliette threw Allison a dirty look. "I wouldn't talk, my friend."

With four brothers, it took more than a little comment like that to bother Allison. "So are you going to be next?" she asked, moving the conversation in a different direction.

"Uh, your wedding is next," Juliette reminded her. "Followed by Curt's and then Brett's."

"Please, you know that's not what I meant."

Courtney didn't see her sister serious about a man anytime

soon. Then again, wedding proposals were spreading as fast as the flu through the family as of late.

Juliette picked up her wineglass as she shook her head. "Nah. I'm thinking Tory. She's been seeing the same guy since October."

At the moment, their second cousin Victoria Sherbrooke, or as her friends and family called her, Tory, sat across the room talking to Anderson Brady, one of the few friends Josh had invited to the wedding. Leah and Juliette talked to Tory far more than she did, so her sister would know their cousin's relationship status. But if Tory was serious about someone she'd been seeing for months, she wasn't acting like it tonight. For most of the reception, she'd been flirting with either Anderson or Josh's cousin.

"Maybe it'll be Alec. Is he seeing anyone?" Courtney was a little surprised when her cousin had said he was coming alone. Although nowhere near as bad as his older brother Trent used to be with women, Alec rarely spent much time single.

Allison shrugged. "If he is, my brother hasn't said anything to me."

The current song ended, and Josh's dad stepped in to be Adalynn's dance partner for the next song. No longer needed on the dance floor, Josh headed in her direction.

Before he sat, he kissed her cheek. "She'd keep me out there all night if she could."

She'd noticed how much the little girl enjoyed dancing. Not only had Josh and his dad danced with Adalynn several times, but she'd also danced with Scott and Jake. When she couldn't get an adult to partner with her, she joined Reese, the next youngest wedding guest.

"Does she take lessons?" Juliette asked. Unlike Courtney, who'd quit after three years, Juliette spent years taking dance classes.

"Not yet. But she's been asking." Josh gestured for a waiter and ordered a coffee.

"Would anyone else like something?" the waiter asked.

"Coffee sounds good," Allison said.

"Another glass of chardonnay," Juliette chimed in.

Courtney could use some caffeine or a bed. She felt as if she hadn't slept in a month. Actually, she'd been exhausted a lot lately. At first, she'd chalked it up to the stress. When the nausea started, Courtney assumed she was getting sick. This morning she hadn't only felt nauseous, but she'd thrown up after eating breakfast. She couldn't remember the last time she'd done that. And it got her thinking.

A quick check of her calendar confirmed her last period had been in December. Even though she was on the pill, her periods were never regular, but rarely did she skip it two months in a row. If her last one had started the day she returned from Hawaii, it was highly likely she should've had one by now. So while Josh picked up his mom at the airport and headed down to Newport, she grabbed a double pack of pregnancy tests from the pharmacy.

Both gave her identical answers. And when they were alone, she'd give Josh the news. How he would react was anyone's guess. They'd casually discussed having children someday, but the conversation hadn't contained a time frame. So the possibility he'd prefer to wait was very real.

Whether he wanted to wait doesn't matter now. "I'll have a cup of tea, please."

With so many tea drinkers in the family, she'd made sure a wide variety of teas were available this evening. When the waiter returned with their drinks, he'd bring the tea chest so she could pick what she wanted. Usually, she preferred chai or Earl Grey, but tonight she'd go with a caffeine-free herbal blend.

Should she tell him as soon as they went upstairs? Or would it be better to wait until they were in bed?

"Josh, isn't your mom married?" Allison's question pulled Courtney's thoughts away from the conversation ahead of her.

The gold mermaid-style evening gown made it easy to locate Scarlett. Earlier in the evening, she'd been sitting with Josh's sister. Now she was practically sitting in Wayne Crawley's lap. Wayne was a close friend of her dad, and she'd known him all her life. A widower, he spent most of his time these days either playing tennis, golfing, or working.

"As far as I know, yes. But with her, who knows."

WHEN THEY ENTERED THEIR ROOM, Courtney had every intention of sitting Josh down and telling him she was pregnant. Josh had very different ideas. No sooner did they close the door than his lips covered hers. While his lips worked at making her forget her name, his hands went about unzipping her dress. By the time they reached the bed, they were both naked, and having a conversation, even one this important, no longer mattered.

Now was a different story.

She'd unpacked her bag when she arrived at Cliff House, so while Josh poured two glasses of champagne, Courtney got the robe hanging in the closet.

"You should have left that in there." Josh smiled and handed her a glass.

She didn't expect to be wearing the robe long, but serious conversations required clothing. "We need to talk." Rather than return to the bed, where Josh might once again distract her, she crossed to the love seat and set down the glass untouched. Wedding or not, alcohol was out for the foreseeable future.

"Sounds like underwear is required."

She watched him walk to where he'd left his clothes. No question about it, her husband had one perfect butt.

"What's on your mind?"

Who was she kidding? Just sitting there in nothing but his underwear, Josh distracted her. You'd think after seeing him in various states of undress so much, it would no longer affect her. But it did.

"You know I haven't been feeling great lately."

In the process of sipping his champagne, he nodded.

"I know why now. I'm pregnant."

Josh's coughing fit stopped her from saying anything else.

"How? Until three weeks ago, we always used a condom."

"That night at my parents', we didn't."

"But you're on the pill."

"I didn't pick up the prescription on time, and I ended up skipping a few days that week. It's not the first time it's happened, and it didn't seem like a big deal because I wasn't having sex."

"When did you find out?"

"This morning. After you left, I went and bought the tests. They both came back positive." She understood his initial surprise and his questions. With those out of the way, it'd be nice if he hinted at how he felt about the news.

"You took two tests."

She nodded.

"And they were both positive?"

"You're not happy about this."

"Of course I am." Josh lifted her onto his lap and kissed her forehead. "I'm surprised as hell but ecstatic." He placed his hand over her stomach. "And I can't wait to meet our son or daughter."

Their discussion brought to mind her interview with Aimee Trainor weeks ago. That night, the woman had asked if she was pregnant. Even claimed there was a rumor going around that she was and her pregnancy was the reason behind their short engagement. Not only had Courtney denied it, she'd thought to herself that one thing she could say with certainty was that she and Josh would never be expecting a child. Turned out even as she'd been denying it, she was already pregnant.

Life could be so unpredictable and full of surprises.

The hand on her stomach inched its way up and covered her breast. "I love you."

Actions sometimes worked better than words. Right now seemed like one of those times.

BOOKS BY CHRISTINA

*Loving The Billionaire, a novella

*The Teacher's Billionaire

*The Billionaire Playboy

*The Billionaire Princess

*The Billionaire's Best Friend

*Redeeming The Billionaire

*More Than A Billionaire

*Protecting The Billionaire

*Bidding On The Billionaire

*Falling For The Billionaire

*The Billionaire Next Door

*The Billionaire's Homecoming

*The Billionaire's Heart

*Tempting The Billionaire

+The Courage To Love

+Hometown Love

+The Playboy Next Door

+In His Kiss

+A Promise To Keep

+When Love Strikes

^Born To Protect

^His To Protect

ABOUT THE AUTHOR

USA Today Best Selling author, Christina Tetreault started writing at the age of 10 on her grandmother's manual typewriter and never stopped. Born and raised in Lincoln, Rhode Island, she has lived in four of the six New England states since getting married in 2001. Today, she lives in New Hampshire with her husband, three daughters and two dogs. When she's not driving her daughters around to their various activities or chasing around the dogs, she is working on a story or reading a romance novel. Currently, she has three series out, The Sherbrookes of Newport, Love on The North Shore and Elite Force Security. You can visit her website http://www.christinatetreault.com or follow her on Facebook to learn more about her characters and to track her progress on current writing projects.

Printed in Great Britain
by Amazon